DINOSAUR VALLEY

DINOSAUR VALLEY

The Archaeologists #1

K.H. KOEHLER

The Monster Factory

Copyright © 2021 by K.H. Koehler

All rights reserved. No part of this publication may be reproduced, stored or transmitted in any form or by any means, electronic, mechanical, photocopying, recording, scanning, or otherwise without written permission from the publisher. It is illegal to copy this book, post it to a website, or distribute it by any other means without permission.

This novel is entirely a work of fiction. The names, characters and incidents portrayed in it are the work of the author's imagination. Any resemblance to actual persons, living or dead, events or localities is entirely coincidental.

Paperback ISBN: 979-8-8692-2532-0
Ebook ISBN: 979-8-8692-2533-7

Cover art and interior design by KH Koehler Design

https://khkoehler.net

No part of this book was created using artificial intelligence.

CONTENTS

1

DISCOVERY

2

EXPLORATION

ABOUT THE AUTHOR

1

DISCOVERY

Where There's Gun Smoke, There's Fire

Dead Horse, Arizona, 1901

"Lay one hand on me, sir, and you will find it lying on the ground next to your head!"

The voice was female, laden with a British accent, and very agitated. It was also coming from a window. The window was on the second floor of Constance's Boarding House, located at the dusty end of Main Street.

Sheriff Sydney Fly, who had been called out because of a disturbance at a nearby saloon, slowed his eight-year-old paint to a trot and turned his head.

"Foreigners, Molly," he told the horse, who had been with him since he'd become sheriff of Dead Horse, a border town deep in the heart of the Arizona Territory. "It's always the foreigners."

The horse tossed her head as if mutually agreeing.

A crash echoed from within the boardinghouse, followed by the sounds of breaking glass...and then followed by a string of curses so bizarre, Syd was certain the Englishwoman was five sheets to the wind.

With a sigh, Syd slid out of the saddle and landed on his boot heels, shook off the layer of dust clinging to his cowhide coat, and straightened his hat. The horse, an opportunist like her owner, immediately took advantage of the watering trough while Syd stomped up the rickety stairs of the slightly leaning structure and knocked two-knuckle-style against the thin wooden door.

"Connie? It's Syd."

Constance, the local proprietress and town madam, yanked the door open seconds later. She looked fit to be tied.

Syd dutifully removed his hat the way his good momma had taught him. Didn't matter who or what she was, Syd was a firm believer in chivalry, and, generally speaking, liked women of all kinds and calibers.

Connie's calico bustle dress emphasized her considerable assets, which legend told had once had the power to draw roughnecks and cowpokes from miles around. Now in her mid-forties, she had her stable of loyal girls doing all the heavy lifting, such as it was. Her face was flushed and pinched—not pretty, exactly, but intense. "I hope you're here for that lime-juicin' jackrabbit, Sheriff. She's doin' a fine job of chasing away my clients!"

"Pardon?" It took him a moment to follow. He was about to inquire further when there was a considerable explosion of what sounded like porcelain from upstairs. It sounded like Connie's lime-juicin' jackrabbit had tossed a whole wash basin set against the far wall.

Muttering a curse, Syd muscled by, crossed the foyer, and took the steps of the boardinghouse two at the time until he reached the upstairs hallway. By then, one of the doors had been flung wide open and a man—he looked like one of Carter Worthington's hired hands—staggered out, his trousers down around his ankles and his hands covering his head. Blood oozed over one eye from an especially deep cut on his forehead.

Syd finally recognized him through the blood. His name was Burt, and he was one of Connie's regulars, but what followed him out was a vision straight out of heaven—or, at the very least, a very interesting version of hell.

The porcelain-slinging, lime-juicin' jackrabbit was a young woman in her early twenties. She was of exceedingly small statue—barely taller than a child, really—with skeeter bites for a bust and frazzled dark blonde hair braided away from a face that Syd could only call feral. She was wearing fancier clothes that he was used to seeing in these parts, even on Connie's stable of girls, and a pair of glasses pushed to the top of her head. She resembled an escapee from an asylum for the insane. That was worrisome enough, but she was also wielding a hybrid weapon of some kind, a double-action long colt/longsword that she currently had aimed at Burt's face. And that pretty much convinced Syd that she was most certainly not a member of Connie's stable.

He hoped to appeal to her better nature—assuming she had one.

"Miss..." Syd began, holding up his hands and glaring at the peculiar weapon, "...miss, I think you should calm down. We can discuss all this down at the sheriff's office..."

He immediately regretted his words when the young woman turned her stormy grey eyes—and the gun/sword weapon combination—on him instead.

"Begging your pardon, *sir*. This...*man*...had every intention of doing unspeakable things to me!"

The little blonde's already agitated face crumpled up into a snarl as she turned back to Burt. "And you." She shook the weapon at him as her voice rose in volume. "You...animal...you *Neanderthal*! Right now, I will not be trifled with!"

She pulled the trigger.

The gun/sword went off with a deafening, cannon-like blast that shook the whole building. Belatedly, Sydney realized the rifle part had been outfitted with something closer to the barrel of an elephant gun. The weapon also kicked like a Sunday mule, and the scattershot took out a whole portion of the wall near Burt's head, giving Connie's boardinghouse an impromptu new window.

Burt let out an expletive, tripped over his trousers, and wheeled backward down the stairs, rolling most of the way. He scrambled to his feet after he hit the bottom and bolted out the door, wrestling with his belt and trousers and screaming blue murder.

"Oh, my," said the blonde, a hand to her throat. Her eyes went wide in her small, catlike face as she turned to Syd with a strangely angelic smile. "I've never fired it before." She said this conversationally. "It works marvelously, doesn't it? Quite the wonder..."

Syd stomped forward and snatched the weapon away. "I think that will be enough, miss."

"Hello?" She tried to grab at it, but Syd, standing more than a foot taller than she, easily kept it out of the range of her grip. Still, she made a valiant effort to jump up and down. Her hair flew in all directions. "That's mine! I made that! Do you know how long I've worked on that? You have no right...!"

"Miss," Syd explained as patiently as he was able to, "I have every right, and I think you need to calm down..."

Her face grew furious once more and her cheeks pinked from rage. "I am no miss and I will *not* calm down! My name is Lady Anna Rutherford and that weapon is very valuable to me!"

"Sheriff!" Constance said, stomping up the stairs, bundles of her hoop skirts in both fists. She looked at the weapon as if she were staring into the face of the devil himself. "I hope you plan on resolving this situation immediately. Who is going to pay for that wall?"

She made a vague gesture toward the damage. "You must arrest this foreigner! My guests downstairs are getting nervous!"

"How dare you!" Lady Anna Rutherford crowed, throwing herself at Connie. Would have gotten her too if Syd hadn't put a hand gently on her arm and restrained her.

"Sheriff, unhand me!" Lady Anna demanded while Connie threw the Englishwoman a cross look.

Syd could hear grumbling from Connie's clientele sitting in the drawing room downstairs. One of Connie's girls stepped out of a boarding room in the hall, dressed only in her knickers and corset, screamed when she saw the hole in the wall, and ducked back inside.

Syd sighed. He had no choice. He emptied the gun/sword of ammunition, tightened his grip around Lady Anna's arm, and hauled her down the stairs despite her wild protests.

"Miss...please! Miss, come with me."

She kicked and screamed like a wildcat, calling on her title, threatening him with the most remarkably stupid punishments—including the Tower of London, whatever that was.

Foreigners...yeah. He'd see if the crazy little blonde with the crazier weapon was still full of piss and vinegar after a night cooling her heels in the town jail!

| 2 |

Siege!

"This is outrageous! I did nothing wrong! Sheriff, if you don't release me immediately, something terrible will happen!" The little blonde's bellyaching went on and on.

Syd set the curious gun/sword down on his desk and studied it. He wished it could tell him its story—because he sure as hell wasn't going to get anything sensible out of the mouth in his jail cell. It was a tremendously complicated piece of work. Syd, who had some experience with mechanical engineering, could see that plainly. It seemed to be made of some kind of alloy, the gun and sword tempered to a shining silver finish and fused together with expert care. Syd was impressed.

In the years before he took up the mantle of sheriff, Syd had worked in his daddy's photography studio, learning the ins and outs of the various box cameras his father had used. His father, in his youth, had been a soldier in the War to Preserve the Union. He'd photographed wounded soldiers for the city newspapers for a wage. In the course of it, he'd also collected a number of fine weapons, all of which had decorated the walls of the studio where Syd had grown up helping his dad. Young Sydney had seen all manner of weapons, but nothing this impressive.

"Sheriff! I demand an audience immediately!"

Syd raised his head. "You shut up, miss!"

"I will *not* shut up! How dare you!"

The blonde started raking her tin cup against the bars of her cell.

Grumbling, Syd started toward the cells. Halfway there, he heard a deep bass rumble and the whole jail rocked slightly, making the lanterns swing from the ceiling and the collection of Union swords on one wall topple over. Syd, used to the frequent blasting from Fossil Mountain, put his arms out and steadied himself while aftershocks rocked the small clapboard building.

Damn that Carter Worthington. The man was a con and a swindler—probably a lunatic, as well. Owner of "Worthington's World of Wonders," a traveling exhibition show, he'd been tearing these hills apart looking for bones and fossil eggs to add to his so-called "prehistoric show."

Syd had experienced just one afternoon of his over-publicized buffoonery, and it had been enough. He'd thought it would be the typical sharp-shooting, roping, riding, and border dramas that were a mainstay of such shows since Buffalo Bill Cody's Wild West show had become *de rigueur*—and he was half-right. There were plenty of stunts and shows. But Worthington wasn't satisfied with horses, bulls, and buffalo. Instead, he exhibited exotic animals from Africa, Asia, and god knew where else. His shows were full of lion tamers and riders on zebras and elephants. There were always a lot of accidents wherever Worthington went, but the man was moneyed, and anyone who so much as breathed wrong in his presence was run out of town.

The Bone Wars had ended. The famous, heated rivalry between paleontologists Edward Drinker Cope and Othniel Charles Marsh had ended a few years ago, both men having gone bankrupt in a rush to blow as many prehistoric bones out of the earth as humanly and financially doable. As a result, the southwest had been opened up to anybody calling themselves an archaeologist, and there was a full-on "bone rush" to exploit what could be yanked out of the ground. Syd had heard the city folk call it "dinosaur fever." Greedy, shady industrialists had been crawling out of the woodwork for years, and that was like ringing the dinner bell for someone like Carter Worthington.

He's going to blow this whole damned town up, Syd thought as he set the swords back on the wall.

Lady Anna, meanwhile, was weaving on her feet and clinging to the bars of her cell. She looked paler than usual. "What is that? *What* is going on?"

"The Worthington crew. They're blasting bones."

"Blasting bones?"

Syd hitched a thumb backward. "Carter Worthington? Of Worthington's World of Wonders? They blast bones from the ground so stupid city folk with money can gawk at them. Makes no sense to me."

"Oh, him." Lady Anna's cheeks piqued as she looked away. "He blasts them to bits. There's nothing left." She turned back to look at Syd. "I take it you don't approve, Sheriff?"

Syd thought about that a moment before answering. "The Navajo say anything taken from the earth should be used to good purpose. Worthington is just making money—so, no."

Was that a look of approval in her ladyship's eyes? Syd couldn't be certain.

"Worthington is a cretin," she explained through a fence of gritted teeth. "I don't doubt he sent that Neanderthal to the boarding-house to get information out of me!"

"Burt?"

"The same." Her face crumpled with determination.

Syd crossed his arms across his burly chest as a thought occurred to him. "Burt couldn't shoot his way out of a sack. Espionage seems a little beyond him." He looked her highness up and down, a smirk ticking one corner of his mouth. "You do know Connie's boardinghouse isn't actually a boardinghouse, right?"

Lady Anna Rutherford looked confused. Then she seemed to think about it a little bit more before her eyes widened behind her round, wire-framed glasses. A sudden, deeper blush crept across her rather becoming, apple-like cheeks. When she wasn't raging like a rabid bull, she was actually quite pretty in an academic sense, Syd noted.

She squared her shoulders as she struggled to maintain her image and composure. "Yes, of course I do. It was quite bloody obvious from the start, but I…well, you see, there were no other accommodations in town. One makes do with what one can."

"Indeed." Syd ran a hand across his mustachioed mouth to keep the smirk there from spreading.

"I'm a worldly woman, Sheriff. I graduated from Cambridge with a degree in the social sciences and studied archaeology under Augustus Henry Lane-Fox Pitt Rivers. I was his star pupil." Lady Anna paused as if Syd should know who that is. "I put forth the theory that certain dinosaurs like Iguanodon were bipedal rather than quadrupedal beasts they are normally displayed as to the Zoological Institute in London…not that *they* were likely to take a woman's word for it."

"I see," he said, not seeing at all. He had no idea what she was prattling on about, but this pretty little bookworm was wildly entertaining. "Now…Lady Anna Rutherford…would you mind telling me exactly what you're doing here? Perhaps you can give me the name of your escort so I may contact her...or him?"

Lady Anna Rutherford's cheeks flamed anew. "My business is my own. And I have no escort—nor do I need one!"

Syd found that a little hard to believe. It was an enlightened era, that was for sure. Women were going to universities, becoming doctors and *archaeologists*...hell, they would probably have the vote in just a few short years. But what woman in this day and age left her home on another continent and sailed to America alone, without an escort?

Only a madwoman.

"Lady Rutherford..." he began once more, intent on asking her a few more questions about her business here, when a rough-looking man stepped into his jail. He looked like another of Worthington's hired men. Lowlifes and criminals, the lot of them.

They were violent, stupid, and loyal. They called themselves Rough Riders, and they acted as paid muscle for anyone who got in Worthington's way. Syd pushed his hat back and was about to ask him his business when the man pulled a rifle from under his coat, took aim, and fired wildly in his direction.

The blast was deafening, but somehow he managed to miss Syd by a mile, taking out a window instead. Syd swore as he turned sideways to minimize himself as a target. The man tried to re-aim, but by then, Syd was upon him.

Syd pulled his service colt but found he was too close to get off an effective shot. Cursing, he drove the butt of the colt into the man's chin, knocking him and the rifle clear out the door of the jail and down the wooden steps to the muddy street of Dead Horse beyond. Outside, several other Rough Riders were waiting on horseback, all armed to the teeth with similar weapons.

"Well, shoot," Syd said and ducked back inside, slamming the door behind him. He moved to one side, which was fortunate, as the door was instantly blasted to pieces and sunlight poured in, along with a chorus of angry voices. Syd's ears buzzed from the onslaught.

"Miss," Syd said, checking his munitions, "I reckon you made someone right angry."

"Those men!" Lady Rutherford shouted and rattled the cell door in her panic. "They've come for me. Let me out of here immediately, Sheriff!"

Normally, Syd would never have taken orders from a prisoner, but under the circumstances, her request made sense. While the Rough Riders busied themselves with reloading their rifles, Syd grabbed the keys off his desk and unlocked the cell to let his prisoner out.

Lady Anna Rutherford immediately started toward the door, but Syd grabbed her by the wrist, wrangling her back, and not a moment too soon as another volley of shots blew a dozen new holes in the wall. "Not advisable, miss."

For the first time since they met, Lady Anna looked truly concerned.

A border town, Syd had kicked around Dead Horse long enough to appreciate the advantage of having a back door. Within seconds, they were standing in the narrow delivery alley that ran behind the jail and every other establishment on Main Street worth its mettle. He could hear the Rough Riders calling for him out in the street. Breathing roughly, he listened to their taunts and jeers.

For Syd, this was virgin territory. The "Wild West," such as it was, was long gone. In these later years, Dead Horse had become the type of town that considered a loose bull in the street the epitome of excitement. Hell, he didn't even have a deputy.

Syd's frustration mounted moment by moment, and he had to do everything in his power not to curse. He turned and put a hand up on the shed that Lady Anna Rutherford was huddled against and eyed his prisoner. "Wanna tell me why Worthington's men are after you?"

Lady Anna's eyes grew wider still and she looked like she might start hyperventilating at any moment. He almost felt sorry for her. Still, he didn't much appreciate being shot at out of nowhere, and despite the immediate dangers, he was going no farther until he got some answers.

"What did you do, miss?"

Lady Anna let out a sharp breath. "*That* is none of your business..."

Her words were cut off by an explosion of new shots as the Rough Riders shot up the remnants of Syd's jail. The air was full of the smell of hell and gun oil.

"I think it is. That's a good jail being shot up!"

She tried to move toward the main street. Whatever else she was—a lady, an archaeologist, a madwoman—she was no coward.

He grabbed her by the arm. "I ought to drag you out by your boot heels and..."

"They don't want *me*!" Lady Anna finally confessed, throwing her hands up. "They want my dinosaur...!"

Syd shook his head. "Excuse me...?"

"...and, let me assure you, Sheriff, they will be getting *him* over my dead body!"

| 3 |

First Bird

The brute of a sheriff looked unconvinced, though his expressive lips twisted slightly beneath his neatly trimmed mustache. Anna could tell he would need a tad more convincing about the importance of her mission.

"Dinosaurs," he guffawed. "All this ballyhoo is because you stole some of ol' Worthington's *bones?*"

"I did no such thing! I am no thief!" Anna stated, crossing her arms over the bodice of her dress. She listened for a moment but noted that the Rough Riders hadn't gone yet. She could hear them stomping around the sheriff's office, looking for them. What to do? It was obvious Sheriff Fly wouldn't believe anything she said until he saw for himself.

Don't trust him, a part of her mind whispered. Don't trust anyone in this country!

Normally, Anna liked to keep her own council, but under these circumstances, she figured it might be best to have an ally—or, at least, someone who might prevent her from being shot dead in the street. Anna peeked around the corner of the door and noted that the Rough Riders had stomped out of the jail.

Turning, she grabbed Sheriff Fly by the hand and started dragging him back toward the boardinghouse, which was only a few establishments down the narrow street from the sheriff's office.

"Hey…" the sheriff complained, but she paid him no mind. She just kept right on running. Once she reached Connie's boardinghouse, she did her best to ignore the sly, interested glances of the men sitting in the foyer and led the sheriff up the stairs and back to her room.

Her reputation was quite ruined already, she reminded herself.

Anna had arrived in America only the week before. It was her first journey on her own with no escort or nanny, and she was immensely proud of herself, despite being sick off the bow of the *Mauretania* for most of it. In New York City, she had arranged transport by train to the Arizona Territory—another first, although, admittedly, she had paid a number of principled-looking gentleman to sit in and act as her escorts along the way to deflect any suspicion on the part of the railroad service.

Still, it was fairly obvious to everyone who bothered to notice such things that she was unaccompanied…unattached. If her parents ever found out she was loitering in the colonies, they would disown her and cut her off from her inheritance, but, as it was, they thought she had sailed to India to stay at her father's estate in Simla. The thought kept her awake at night, for it wouldn't be long now before they discovered her ruse.

Considering her time-sensitive mission, she hadn't the time— or, indeed, even the inclination—to contrive a convincing story on reaching Dead Horse. Soon after checking into Connie's boardinghouse, she had shoved her cot to the far wall so she could make use of the room's limited space. She had moved the lonely little writing desk to the center and had purchased a milled board to balance upon it.

Her scientific equipment lay scattered upon it, untouched since the sheriff had taken her to jail. Her mineral deposit test kits, her archeology technician's tool box, a portable microscope, a dairy centrifuge she had managed to purchase locally, and all her maps, notebooks, and reference materials. And there, in one corner of the room, was a large bamboo birdcage under a drop cloth.

She knew the sheriff was confused the moment he stepped into her room. Probably, he expected to see frocks and baubles everywhere he looked, but Anna had outgrown such trivialities while still a lean young girl. Indeed, she had spent much of her young adulthood pursuing scientific matters, which her father found amusing and her mother abhorrent. Her education had worried them. It was certain to worry any suitor who took an interest in her, which was why she avoided them. In fact, she had arrived on the shores of the colonies with armfuls of scientific equipment crammed into steamer trunks and just two traveling dresses—a fact that would have caused her very proper lady's maid back home to have a fainting spell, if she knew.

She supposed she should have been as appalled as everyone else in her life, but in the last week, she had known a freedom she had never experienced before. For the first time ever, Lady Anna Rutherford understood the draw of adventure.

She went to one corner where the floorboards were loose and pried up a board. From the hidey-hole beneath, she withdrew her backup dress, which she had unceremoniously used to cushion her precious treasure. Turning, she presented her guest with her brother Edmond's journal and his collection of letters, all tied neatly together with twine.

The sheriff was tall and well built, young and handsome in that American way (if one was inclined to such things). He was minimally more groomed than other cowboys that Anna had seen, his chocolate-brown, collar-length hair tucked behind both ears and his shirt fairly wrinkle-free. His eyes were bright and keen and of a peculiar type of greenish-blue that seemed to change with his moods. There was grime under his fingernails and sweat stains down the back of his shirt, but since arriving on these shores a week ago, Anna had grown accustomed to the rough and tumble American lifestyle.

The sheriff—he'd said his name was Syd—looked unimpressed. "A journal?"

"Read it. And the letters, too." She hesitated. "You do read?"

"Yes, actually," Sheriff Syd responded, somewhat tersely. He opened the journal, which wasn't long and chronicled her brother's latest adventure, and started perusing the pages, the illustrations…the *evidence*. Then he moved to the letters. She saw his posture stiffen.

"Yes," she agreed. "It's incredible. And no, it's not fiction. My twin brother Edmond is something of an explorer—an adventurer, if you will…unlike me." She clenched her teeth as the old familiar pain returned. "My brother has always been a bit of a…a black sheep, if you will. He doesn't hold to my father's rigid ways or the way he was groomed him to take over the estate. Edmond was the one who went exploring while I stayed at home to read about it."

She paused and sighed as she recalled all her old regrets. "Edmond has always wanted to fly in the face of my father's ways, so he came here to the colonies to make an independent life for himself. My father cut him off for it. And then…well, Worthington happened."

Anna closed her eyes, recalling her brother's frantic letters, the exciting, wonderful journal Edmond had sent her, so full of incredible, impossible things. But on the heels of that was always the sadness, the dread…the feeling that things had so quickly gone sideways for him.

"Edmond is an accomplished hunter—Africa, India. He quickly became fascinated with Worthington. He considered it a boon to meet and associate with him. And that's when things began to go very wrong."

Syd, resting his hip against her desk, leaned forward a little. "Go on."

Anna found it almost impossible to. "Worthington promised Edmond a share in his traveling show for Edmond's services hunting new wildlife. Of course, my brother readily agreed. He wrote me letter after letter, telling me about his *great adventure*." She indicated the letters. "Finally, he told me he was riding off for this valley where the most fantastic creatures had managed to survive. He said it was in the very heart of the Sonora, an ancient oasis. He said almost no one knew of its existence, and practically no one knew how to get there."

She hesitated as worry nipped at her mind and turned her stomach. "Mind you, Sheriff, I was never my father's champion, but on this we agreed. I'd read enough American newspapers and accounts to know how dangerous Worthington is, but Edmond left with a caravan before Father or I could write him back and warn him of Worthington's duplicity. Soon after…well, Edmond's letters stopped. I haven't heard from him since, and Worthington won't speak of what's happened to my brother, but I know whatever it is…it's terrible."

Syd glanced up at her, his face carefully blanked of emotion. She could tell he was a man who played his cards very close to his vest. "You think he's still in this valley…with these creatures." He indicated the journal where Edmond had made many elaborate sketches of the animals he had spotted there.

"I know he is. And I know that valley is real," Anna explained. "I have proof."

It was time, she decided. She turned to the corner where she kept the birdcage and reached for the drop cloth, pulling it smoothly away.

Syd started at the sight of the creature inside.

"I bought this off a Navajo brave soon after arriving here. I call him Archie."

The creature squawked and hissed, jumping from perch to perch. It was the size of a pigeon, and clearly bird-like in appearance with bronze feathers painted with iridescent blue chevron highlights that glimmered under the dim, spotty electric lighting in the room. But it was clearly not a bird. Its face was strangely reptilian, and its beak full of tiny, sharp teeth. Additionally, its large, awkward wings bore almost lizard-like claws, and its feathered tail was long and moved in a snake-like fashion from side to side.

Syd carefully approached the cage.

The creature hissed crossly.

Syd flinched, stopped, took a deep breath, and swore in a most ungentlemanly way.

Archie tilted his head and squeaked in response.

"His real name is Archaeopteryx. It means 'first bird,'" Anna explained. "And I promise you, he isn't nearly as fearsome as he seems. In fact, he's quite tame."

"Weird looking bird."

"Archie isn't a real bird. He's a dinosaur who's in a transitional form between feathered dinosaurs and modern birds. And, yes, before you ask, there are more where he came from. A whole valley of them, in fact."

Syd leaned away from Archie, then pushed his hat back on his head and scratched his head. It was obvious to her that there was no longer any doubt that he believed her. "And why, exactly, do you have…Archie?"

Anna went to the cage and unlatched the little door. Archie used his clawed wings to climb to the top of the cage and take off, gliding awkwardly around the small room before landing on Anna's shoulder, where he squeaked. She reached up to give him a few crumbs of biscuit from a dish near the cage. He warbled in gratitude as he wolfed down the crumbs.

"Archie is my bargaining chip, you see," Anna explained. "He's going to help me find a scout to take me to the valley, Sheriff…and to my brother."

The Man with the X-ray Eyeglasses

El Paso, Texas, a few days earlier

Appearances were everything. Adam Bell knew that intrinsically. Having grown up in a workhouse in the East End of London, he knew the base value of innate beauty—a smile, a nod, a sly, well-inserted word or two. For just over two decades, it had been Adam's stock and trade, bread and butter.

There were four local yokels sitting around the green felt card table. Adam sat with his back to the wall while he graciously lost hand after hand of five-card draw. At the moment, he had three oil-stained cards in his hand and the big cowboy across from him was wearing a jackpot grin.

"You a preacher?" the big cowboy asked.

"Not last I checked, mate," Adam answered while he selected two more cards off the pile.

The cowboy looked him up and down. "Then why you dressed like that...mate?"

Adam wore a black pencil-neck suit and white paper collar, his dark hair carefully oiled back over his ears. At twenty-five, he remained smoothly clean-shaven, and a pair of colored, oval pince-nez sat squarely on his long, straight nose. He had never favored the cowboy hats the colonials wore and chose instead to wear a simple derby.

"You look like a preacher or some sissy politician."

"I assure you I am neither, sir," Adam answered.

"You sound funny. Hey, Lou, you think sissy boy here sounds funny?"

"He sure do. He thinks he's the King of England," one of the big cowboy's cohorts laughed.

"England!" the big cowboy chortled. "That's where they got them clocks and rivers and shit." He got up and floundered an elaborate bow meant to look like…something. "Hey, barkeep," he called to the bar area, "get this sissy some tea and crumpets!"

Adam's smile never slipped. "If you're buying, sir, then I'd much prefer a bourbon neat."

"Didn't know no English drank bourbon. Shoot, you probably think it's piss water. You ever play poker, son?" The cowboy sat down.

Adam could feel the tension mounting in the air around him, but he was an old hand at this and didn't so much as blink. "In London, we play Gleek."

The cowboys laughed childishly over that and started making all kinds of inappropriate jokes using the word. The big one pushed his winnings into the middle of the green felt card table, challenging Adam to follow suit. "Ante up, *King*."

Adam fixed his glasses. He'd made them himself in London during his short stint as a confidence man and gentleman thief. It wasn't a career he had favored on those shores. Too many things could go wrong, the King's law was hard on men like himself, and Adam was not a man who favored a stretch in an English prison. Still, the glasses had been well worth all the trouble they'd taken to make. Able to bend light in just such a way, they allowed Adam to see through most solid objects. For instance, the big cowboy had four of a kind.

Adam moved his winnings to the center of the table, then added his gold pocket watch for good measure. The cowboy's grin widened at that. Utilizing the sleight of hand he'd perfected while living on the streets of the East End, he deftly liberated a few choice cards from his sleeve and soon had a royal flush to lay down.

The cowboys stopped laughing after that.

"Well, I'd say that was beginner's luck," Adam said, rising to gather his winnings into his coat pocket.

"He's a cheater," one of the cowboys stated emphatically. "I saw him winking at that girl up there." He hooked his thumb backward at the saloon girls standing in a row on the balcony, waving to potential marks. "He's workin' with them!"

"I assure you, sir, there was no winking..." Adam explained as he quickly and efficiently filled his pockets.

But by then, all the men at the table were getting up. As he was not exactly being the brawler type, Adam thought it best to abscond into the night that was his longtime friend. But as he turned around, he spotted the barkeep, who had a double-barrel shotgun pointed right at his head.

"We don't like cheaters here, boy," the barkeep said.

Adam started working his verbal magic, making all kind of explanations, but that was quickly cut off. He had to duck as the gun went off with an explosive blast that left his ears ringing.

"Bloody hell," he breathed from his refuge under the table. Bloody Americans!

The blast had taken out one of the batwing doors. But by then, Adam had his route all picked out. While everyone recovered, he crawled from under the table and bolted up the stairs to the rooms above the saloon. Several of the doxies squealed as he made a bee-line toward the nearest door.

Coitus interruptus had never meant so much as it did now as Adam zipped past the couple in bed and dove for the open window. Hooking an arm around the casting, he turned and swung himself up onto the cheap tin roof with all the dexterity of a monkey. Having grown up on the streets, he knew how to pull a runner, and having spent a short stint as a confidence man in a carnival had helped hone his many talents. From there, it was just a few hops across the noisy tin roofs to the blacksmith's next door.

The blacksmith was busy re-shoeing a tackled-up horse for a customer. Adam dropped down into the saddle of the client's horse, grabbed up the reins, and turned the horse's head, ripping its hoof right out of the blacksmith's grip.

"Hey, I wasn't finished!" the blacksmith yelled.

"Sorry, mate," Adam said as he took off at a canter down the street.

Shots followed him for several hundred meters. He ducked and zigzagged to miss the lot of them, though when he glanced over one shoulder, he noticed with some disappointment the trail of cards he was leaving behind. They were fluttering out of his sleeves like a breadcrumb trail.

"Ah, hell." He spurred the horse on until they had cleared Main Street and hit the stretch of dirt road that led away to the train station. Coaches, men on horseback, and even a flivver zipped past him, but he didn't slow the horse until he was certain he wasn't being followed.

Adam checked his pocket watch. He was behind by two minutes. Ahead, he could hear the train passing through El Paso as it cut its slow, lumbering way through the Arizona Territory on its way to San Francisco. The air horn blasted through the valley. Adam leaned tight against his getaway horse as he headed toward the track.

At least the horse was young and able to keep up. Within seconds, he was racing alongside a cargo car, the centrifugal force of the train ripping at his clothes and hair.

Behind him, a shot rang out, glancing by his ear. Looking back, he recognized a couple of the cowboys from the saloon. They had picked up his trail and were following by more than a few meters, yet far too close for Adam's comfort. They had their weapons in hand, but as they were ahorse, they were having trouble aiming effectively. Adam slapped the horse's flank with the reins, urging him on. The horse snorted and poured on the speed.

The roaring train grew closer.

Now the cowboys were shouting obscenities at him, ordering him to stop or they would shoot him—which they planned to do if he did, in fact, stop.

"I really don't think so, mates." Adam jerked the horse's head closer to the train. The old service train thundered alongside him. The wheels rumbled and growled inches away. Now or never, he thought, and jumped.

He was airborne for one terrifying second before latching onto a cargo door. Due to malnutrition in his youth, Adam was a slight, agile man of medium height and was able to claw onto the side of the train with little trouble. Wind ripped at him, threatening to tear from the train and cast him backward like flotsam. It snatched his derby right off his head, but somehow he managed to hang on for dear life.

At least he'd timed things right. The train began to slow as it reached the bend in the river and the tracks diverted. Adam took the opportunity to clamber up the door to the roof of the cargo car. The cowboys, meanwhile, raced on past, following the horse off into the woods. Adam slowly but surely cleaved his way across the roof to the back of the train where the travel and luggage cars were located. He dropped down to the caboose just as the train began to increase its speed once more as it hit the straight rails.

Grinning, he turned on the caboose, hooked an arm around the rail, leaned way out, and waved to the cowboys off in the wood. "Good day, gentlemen!" he called and added, "Consider yourselves privileged. You lot were just ripped off by the descendent of Robin of Locksley!"

He was still congratulating himself on a job well done as he slid the door open and let himself into the dining car.

That's when he stopped. Standing before him was a wanker in a black suit and overcoat, holding a Derringer that he had trained on Adam's chest. "Adam Bell?" the mysterious man said with a sly, satisfied smile. "Pinkerton Agent Reginald King." He flipped back his coat to show a badge. "I'm afraid you're under arrest."

***

Less than twenty-four hours later, Adam found himself sharing a cell with a drunken Indian in a dingy little way station on the cusp of the Arizona Territory. The Pinkerton had unceremoniously dropped his sorry hindquarters there while he visited the telegraph station to call in the warrant, but Adam wasn't planning on waiting around.

Using the heels of his boot, he busily smashed at the bricks at the back of the cell while the drunken old Indian lay on the bunk opposite, gurgling in his sleep. In less than an hour, the mortar had given out and the bricks had started falling away, revealing the hidey-hole he'd been told was waiting for him.

The Indian startled awake and sat up on his bunk. "What you doing? Never get out of here that way, you crazy white boy."

"That's what you think, sir," Adam said, giving the wall one last kick. The hole, now large enough to pass his hand into, yielded up the envelope he'd been told was there.

"Got any whiskey there, crazy white boy?"

"No, sorry, mate," Adam said, slipping the envelope into his inside jacket pocket.

"How 'bout some smokes? Crazy white boys always have smokes."

Adam was passing the old Indian one of his hand-rolled cigarettes just as the Pinkerton returned, an annoyed expression on his face.

"It seems there's been some misunderstanding," Agent King said, using a key to unlock the cell door. "I spoke to your employer, Mr. Worthington. It seems the charges in El Paso have been dropped. You're free to go, Mr. Bell."

"Crazy white boy have some big magic," the old Indian said, enjoying Adam's smoke.

Adam patted the old man's shoulder. "You have no idea."

Adam sashayed out of the cell. "Thank you, Agent King. It's been a pleasure." He tipped an invisible hat to the man as he marched past him and out into the bright, sunshiny day. He stood in the dusty streets, his face turned up toward the brutal but beautiful Arizona sun. Never underestimate the almighty American dollar, he thought, or men in high places like Carter Worthington.

Minutes later, a coach pulled up, surrounded by a cloud of desert sand. The coach was mostly full, with luggage tied to the top. All the same, the coachman jumped down and opened the door for him as if he were royalty.

"Tucson," the coachman said. "Mr. Worthington is waiting for you, sir."

"Very good, my man." Adam clapped the coachman on the shoulder before boarding the coach. He kept a hand on the envelope in his pocket, his ticket to a better life. "Very good, indeed."

| 5 |

Village of the Damned

The village was spare and mean, a lonesome tract of dusty land on the far side of the river that reminded Anna a little too much of the East End of London, where the poor and desperate gather by the river under bridges. She had not had many occasions to visit that part of the city—indeed, her father called it "unbecoming and dangerous"—but the few times her family's coach had passed along the borders, she vividly recalled the dirty, hungry faces of the children, the doxies lurking in the alleyways, the drunks in the gutters. The eyes. Small and feral, tracking her family with bitter desperation. Her mother never said anything in those instances, simply sitting on the bench beside Anna, clutching her throat as if an invisible knife were pointed at it.

Anna thought about that now as they rode into the Indian village. It was little more than a collection of wigwams with cooking fires pouring from them. Bleary-eyed drunks sprawled in the dirt and unsupervised children chased each other around, while dogs with their ribs showing pawed through piles of garbage. The young adults—Braves they were called, as she understood it— sat around smoking or talking in conspiratorial whispers amongst themselves as if afraid to raise their voices. All of them looked broken and beaten. The cost of colonization. After relocation to these remote patches of uninhabitable land, the native people had simply given up.

Sheriff Sydney rode through confidently enough on his paint, with Anna on a bay gelding behind him. Dogs yipped around the horse's feet, making it shy and snort. She clung to her mount, jiggling dangerously as the weight of their gear jerked her horse this way and that. The birdcage under the drop cloth on the horse's left flank jangled, and Archie let out a concerned twitter.

Sorry, my little friend, she thought.

There had been horses on her father's estate, of course, but she had never been allowed to ride—not like Edmond. Her health, her mother said. Riding might cause her too much excitement. She could gain a brain fever and die. As a result, she had spent most of her childhood and young adulthood locked away in her father's observatory or lost in his vast library of books.

Anna had read a great deal about riding, and she was attempting to apply that knowledge now in a practical manner. She only wished she didn't feel like she was going to fall off her mount any moment.

"This way, miss…eh, Lady Anna," Sydney said, leading a winding, muddy path through the filthy children and animals.

"Are you all right up there?" He sounded genuinely concerned.

She was starting to feel dizzy from the relentless sun, and her stomach growled, reminded her that she hadn't eaten since midday yesterday.

"It's Anna," she said. "Call me Anna. Please."

I am not that person in the coach, she told herself. *I am not Lady Anna. Just Anna.* The idea of pure anonymity appealed to her immensely.

They came to a stone circle with a hut in the center that seemed to be made of twigs and leaves. It was bigger than the other wigwams, with herbs and little figures of wood and clay animals hanging from a wire from the roof and a foul-smelling smoke pouring from a crude tin chimney.

Sydney dismounted, and Anna followed suit.

A child raced up to her, carrying some kind of wooden doll. He kept pointing to it and babbling in Navajo.

"Yes," Anna answered in confusion, kneeling down for the child's benefit. She had very little experience with children. "It's a very nice doll."

"It's a corn poppet," Sydney explained. His mouth quirked up in one corner in a most frustrating way that told her that he knew more about the ways of these people than she ever would, even if she lived here for years. "They use them to cast curses on white people they don't like."

"Oh!" Anna said, not sure whether to believe him or not. She stumbled up and backed away from the child, who was brandishing the doll in her face. "Oh, my!"

Sydney laughed at her discomfort and said something to the child in Navajo. The child turned to him, and he tossed the child a few coins in exchange for the doll.

"He was trying to sell it," Anna said grumpily, cross with the way that Syd was teasing her.

"Big magic," Syd said, tucking the doll away before lifting the flap of buffalo hide that acted as the door to the wigwam. He indicated that she should go first.

Anna stayed exactly where she was, a little confused and still very cross with the sheriff. She didn't like being teased. Other children had teased her unmercifully when she was a girl. It never got any easier.

"It was only a joke," Syd sighed. "Here, take the doll."

"I don't want the doll!" she stated impetuously, then re-thought her outburst. She was acting very spoiled and imperial, just like her parents would have liked, and that was not acceptable. That was not who she was. Not anymore. Angrier with herself than with Syd, she snatched the doll from his hand.

"Fine. I need all the big magic I can get." Only then did she look dubiously at the little hut. "Your friend lives here?"

Syd's half smile twisted slightly at the edges, making his mustache bob. "He does. Come on, now. And bring Archie."

Inside, the atmosphere of the hut was almost crushingly close, and the sickly sweet stench of some kind of burning herb made Anna sneeze three times. Syd turned to an old, grey-haired Indian man sitting on the ground, staring into a burning bowl of leaves. Despite his long hair and the leather bandanna he wore, his clothes were modern white man clothes and similar to Syd's. He even wore a crushed-down fedora with an eagle feather in it.

"Tacoma," Syd said. "This is Lady Anna. She's come all the way from England to talk to you."

Never one to shirk in the face of new company—or a new challenge—Anna set Archie's cage down on the dirt floor and stepped forward. "London, specifically," she explained, offering her hand. Despite the rude conditions, she had no desire to appear inhospitable. "Greetings, Mr. Tacoma."

The old Indian didn't take her hand. He just turned his seamed face up to hers. "Another bone blaster, Syd?" He spoke perfect English. "You know better than to bring them here."

Syd dropped down to the floor in a crouch and produced a bottle of whiskey. "No...well, yes, in a way. But Lady Anna is unlike any bone blaster you're ever likely to meet."

Anna lifted an eyebrow at his admission. It was almost a compliment.

Syd cleared his throat with embarrassment. "This little lady is more interested in *living* dinosaurs. Show him, Anna."

Anna sank slowly to the dirt floor, trying to keep her skirts from becoming unduly crumpled. She un-sheeted the cage and Archie immediately woke up, dropped his wing, which was covering his face, and started hopping from perch to perch, making a warbling noise.

Tacoma's eyes, once faded and faraway, suddenly danced with light. "One of the Old Ones!"

"You can say that."

Tacoma raised his hands to the cage as if he were beseeching a god. "How did you come by this?"

Anna watched Archie dance around excitedly for her. "I bought it from one of your own Braves who came into town to sell his wares," she explained. "He was selling Archie for medicine…"

"But you knew better."

Anna nodded. "I've studied archeology. He's certainly an Old One, as you put it."

Archie seemed to agree and started twittering to her.

She took a deep breath before delivering the *coup de gras*. "I need to find out where he came from. I need to return him to his home, Mr. Tacoma."

Tacoma looked at Anna, then Syd, then Anna once more. He seemed surprised. "What about the Brave who sold him to you? Why not go to him?"

"I have no idea where he is. And, anyway, I want to do this. I want to take Archie home." She did not state why.

Still, Tacoma gave her a skeptical look. She could not blame him for that. The way the white men had treated Tacoma's people…well, she would have been skeptical herself. "If you sell him to me, I shall take him home…"

"That won't work," she immediately blurted out as her panic—and her desperation—began to rise. "I mean to launch my own expedition, Mr. Tacoma. It's vitally important that I do so!"

Of course he assumed, as a white woman, that she wanted to steal more dinosaurs like Archie. "Are you always so forward, Miss Anna?"

"You don't know the half of it," Syd answered, taking a swig of the bottle before passing it to Tacoma. "This little lady would wrestle a buffalo into the dust to get what she wants."

Anna ignored Syd's crude remark. "I'm simply on an important mission." Despite her best intentions, her voice began to rise in panicked octaves. "It's important that I find the place where this creature came from."

Tacoma drank down a swallow of Syd's whiskey before rubbing his sleeve across his lips. "Dil Bii 'Ndzisgaii." He grinned with crooked, nicotine-stained teeth at that. "Blood Valley."

Anna tried not to flinch. "If that's what you're calling it, then, yes. I mean to launch an expedition to Dil Bii 'Nd...Blood Valley. Can you guide me?"

Tacoma laughed at that and threw a handful of fresh herbs into his burning bowl. The fire sprang up briefly, along with a plume of bitter smoke. "And why would you want to go there, eh? That place is death."

Anna felt a stab of panic. To come so far and then to be turned away...

"I have to go there. I have no choice."

"There's always a *choice.*"

Anna swallowed as her desperation edged up a notch. One way or another, she had to get to this Blood Valley. "I have money. You could name your price."

"Maybe no money is worth going to Blood Valley." Tacoma offered her shrewd, narrow eyes. "And maybe no white woman belongs there."

She bit her lip. She had to work on not bursting out into sobs in front of this man and making a fool of herself. Did he want her to beg? To get down on her knees?

"I'll pay whatever it takes. I'll give you whatever you want...but, please, I have to go to Blood Valley."

"So you can steal more of the Old Ones," Tacoma said with a wicked gleam in his eyes. "The Englishmen are no different than any white men..."

"You don't understand!" Anna shouted at last, a tear escaping her eye and racing down her cheek. "I have to find my brother, Edmond! I have to bring him home!"

At last, Tacoma looked interested in her plight. She had planned on keeping her reasons to herself, but she saw that was quite impossible at this point.

"Explain," Tacoma said. "And maybe...just maybe...we will have an accord."

Taking a deep breath, she began her story. "My brother—my twin brother, Edmond—was lost to your Blood Valley only last year. He went there, as you say, to steal the Old Ones. I'm not proud of that, Mr. Tacoma, but there you have it. Then he disappeared, and no one has seen him since. I have written authorities...lawmen...but no one is willing to help me. They all assume Edmond is dead. Edmond is not dead!"

Tacoma was silent a long moment as he stared into the crackling fire. "One might call that divine justice." He nodded toward Archie. "He tried to take that which was not his. God saw fit to punish him."

How could she make him understand? Was there any way to appeal to his sense of decency?

"I don't know the ways of God," she admitted, her heart breaking into tiny pieces inside of her. "I don't even know if I believe…and I have no interest in taking dinosaurs from their natural habitat. All I know is that my brother is missing and I need to find him, to save him. My parents disowned him. No one cares that he's out there except me."

Finally, after what felt like an eternity, he said, "Tell me more."

She told Tacoma every last detail about Edmond's expedition, which had been financed by Carter Worthington, though Worthington refused to comment on what had become of his men, despite an almost endless stream of letters on her part. She showed him Edmond's journal and the letters. Near the end, she swallowed hard against the knot of tears in her throat.

"I'll beg if I must, Mr. Tacoma. I'll give you anything you ask. Even though Edmond is missing, I know he's alive. I'm his twin and I can feel him. I can *find* him." She paused as she swallowed and rubbed the tears from her eyes with her sleeve. "Once there, I promise to let Archie go. I swear it on my soul. But the truth is, I need a guide to help me across the desert, and I hope beyond all hope that that guide is you, Mr. Tacoma."

| 6 |

The Homecoming

Tucson, Arizona

Carter Worthington, standing in his posh caravan, held his pocket watch in one hand and stated empirically, "You're late, Mr. Bell."

Like most Americans, Worthington was caustic and impatient. Adam wasn't especially surprised by that, but it did make him pause as he stepped into the fine, spacious caravan with its wainscoted walls, leather lounges, and cosmopolitan paintings on the walls. A pair of twin Gibson girls shared a settee in one corner, sipping champagne and giggling between themselves. Dolly and Molly, if he wasn't mistaken, a pair of former coochie dancers that Worthington employed as mascots for his traveling show. They decorated his posters and fliers and had even done a short, promotional Edison film for him. It was rumored Worthington worked them off the clock, as well.

"Oi," Adam complained. "I got hung up."

The twins giggled and started whispering behind their champagne glasses about how cute Adam was, how they wanted him to come sit by them. One crooked her finely painted fingertip at him. He ignored them and turned his full attention on his boss.

"You didn't say nothing about no bleedin' *Pinkertons*," Adam complained grumpily. He brushed invisible lint off his greatcoat sleeve.

"They didn't keep you, did they?"

"That's not the point, Worthington. I don't like surprises like that." He didn't add that he was wanted in Arizona for at least three counts of larceny. The sooner they got the bloody hell out of the Arizona Territory the better, as far as Adam was concerned. But he wasn't the boss, and he had to remind himself that this was the price he paid for attaching himself to a traveling show. Despite the relative anonymity it offered him, sometimes he wound up criss-crossing territories that would happily see him hanging from a gallows pole.

Even though Worthington had his men doing the bone-blasting throughout the Arizona and New Mexico Territories, his show only did the circuit around the bigger cities where all the money was. This week, it was Tucson. Next week, it was Phoenix, and then the week after they would be moving farther west to Albuquerque, where Adam could finally breathe easier.

While Worthington whispered to his girls, Adam went to the wet bar and poured himself a two-finger whiskey, neat, downing it in one gulp while the twins oohed and aahed his way like simpering idiots. At least Worthington had posh whiskey, he reminded himself, analyzing the dregs of his glass. There was something to be said about that.

When it became apparently that Adam wasn't moving from his spot, Dolly, the saucier of the twins, got up and sashayed to him, draping herself half over him while she poured him another whiskey from the decanter. Adam stiffened, and Worthington laughed at the display.

"Oh, my poor dear, I hate to say it, but you chose the wrong tree to bark up."

Dolly looked confused.

Adam unwound her arm and moved to one side where a number of dramatic posters hung on the wall under glass. They chronicled the sometimes problematic rise of Worthington's World of Wonders. Most featured lurid illustrations of lion-tamers commanding legions of big predatory cats, and trick riders riding wild elephants and buffalo.

Much like Buffalo Bill's Wild West Show, Worthington's World of Wonders had risen quickly in popularity by giving the audience something they had never seen before and showing them a world that most regular people had only ever read about in Edgar Rice Burroughs novels or heard stories about on their grandpappies' knees. Worthington never stopped adding or altering his shows to greater effect.

The man spent his days wheeling, dealing, and expanding his exhibits, and his nights gambling away funds in the nearby casinos or spending them on floozies. He could be found any night of the week with a glass of champagne in one hand and a couple of chorus girls in the other—which is how Adam first encountered the man several years ago. Worthington was impressed by Adam's grifting skills and X-ray eyeglasses and had immediately put him in charge of his security detail.

"Carter, we're almost dry!" the other twin cried from the settee.

"Yes, m'dears." Worthington hurried to fetch a fresh bottle of champagne off the wet bar and carried it to the settee with Dolly all over him like a fur stole. Adam couldn't understand it. The man was short and portly, and the cut of his clothes made him look like a human penguin. He was white-haired and jowly, with a soft baby face completely at odds with his sly, hawk-like eyes. He was also an insufferable, egocentric lunatic. Adam could only assume the women he attracted were there for the smell of cold, hard cash. It certainly wasn't his personality or wit, of which he had none.

"So, where is it?" Worthington demanded to know in a cold tone of voice, bypassing any pleasantries with Adam as he poured the girls fresh drinks.

Adam whipped out the envelope and tossed it unceremoniously to his desk. "Can't say if it's accurate."

"It's accurate," Worthington sniffed.

The girls went back to cooing over their champagne while Worthington returned to his desk, liberating a sheet of paper from the envelope. He leaned forward, his hands braced on the ink blotter, and unfolded what seemed to be a hand drawn map. He held down the corners with stones and small prehistoric skulls from the collection on his desk. "Men have died for this map, Bell," he proclaimed, eyeing it keenly. "They have fought and bled for it. The Pinkertons went through hell to get it."

"Aye, and I went to prison for it," Adam reminded him, setting down his empty whiskey glass with a thunk.

"For one day, Bell."

"It was a long day. And I don't do prison!" Adam sniffed.

"When you see what this map brings, you will understand it's important."

"So, it's a treasure map. Big bloody deal."

"It's more than that. It's worth more than any map to any legendary treasure." Worthington tapped it and grinned up at him. "With this map, we can find Dil Bii ' Ndzisgaii. The legendary Blood Valley. I can wipe Buffalo Bill off the face of the planet."

His eyes lit up with a fire that Adam usually saw in insane asylum inmates. "Who cares about trick riders on horses? What if a girl could glide in on a pterodactyl?"

The twins giggled at that. Adam had no idea what the hell Worthington was on about, not that it deterred the man. He continued by saying, "The old Indian who drew it staked his life on this location. He died for it."

Adam's uneasiness, which he had been experiencing since the beginning of this whole ordeal, continued to grow. He poured himself another drink. "How did he die?"

Worthington's smile never slipped. "He was unlucky."

Adam decided he'd very much like to get out of the caravan as soon as possible. He swallowed down the whiskey. "My money?" He'd been extremely patient up to this point. He wanted to get back to his usual position of head of show security. It put him out of the sight of patrons and well out of Worthington's way—which was just fine by him. The less he had to do with his boss, the better.

"After you go to Dead Horse," Worthington said, folding up the map.

Adam blinked. "Bloody hell...that wasn't our *deal*..."

"The deal's changed, Mr. Bell."

Spikes of outrage needled Adam. He thought about taking out his gun and beating Worthington to a bloody pulp, except Worthington surrounded himself with some pretty unsavory types. There were Rough Riders everywhere, including a wall of serious muscle standing outside his trailer. He'd never make it out alive, not even with his usual bag of tricks.

Worthington eyed him as if he could read his mind. "You don't want to do anything rash, Mr. Bell. Men like yourself don't often survive prison. Now, the job: Take as many men as you need. I want you to disrupt the Rutherford Expedition, which shall be launching in two day's time from Dead Horse. Be creative. You're a descendant of that Robin of Locksley character, aren't you? I'm sure you'll find a way."

"I should kill you now," Adam said.

Worthington never so much as flinched. "You're a wanted man, Mr. Bell." Worthington's smile grew by inches, a predatory smirk that rivaled the creatures in his show. "It would behoove you to stay in my good graces."

* * *

"Son of a bitch," Adam said as he stomped up the stairs of the box office caravan. All of the employee caravans were parked well off the thoroughfare in a privately sectioned part of the fairgrounds. Over fifty shanty caravans, circus wagons, and various tents were set up for Worthington's workers, creating its own little city on the move, and for the past five years, Adam had called the setup home.

"Son. Of. A. Bitch!" He slammed the door of the caravan so hard, all of the glass in the tiny portal windows rattled in their frame.

Inside, William Sharp, Worthington's circus impresario, was carefully pouring his crooked numbers into a large, leather-bound ledger. Adam leaned against a wall, crossed his arms over his chest, and bowed his head. "I'm going to kill that wanker."

"Uh-huh," William answered, not looking up. He rubbed at the side of his face with his fountain pen before dipping it into the inkwell. "That's one way to not get paid, Adam."

"Put a bullet in his bloody head. Drag him behind wild horses!"

William looked up, his round spectacles flashing as he offered Adam a sympathetic smile. He was a young man of medium height and build, always neat in his suit and paper collar. Dust and dirt seemed to abhor William. Part of that was likely due to the fact that he seldom stepped outside the caravan. He spent most of his days, and some of his nights, cooking Worthington's books.

He smiled wryly. "You know, that would be a waste of good bullets and horses."

"The man's a bloody swindler!"

William pointed his pen at Adam. "Kettle, meet pot. Rumor is, a few days ago you were in prison for him."

Adam waved it away. "Only briefly." He poured himself a fresh whiskey from the wet bar and went on to recount his adventures over the last week, concluding with the details of his newest "mission," such as it was.

William managed to look surprised. "Oh, my. Lady Anna Rutherford's expedition. I just read about that in today's newspaper." He dug through the untidy stack of papers on his desk before coming up with the *Tucson Star* and flipping through the top pages. "'Lady Ann Rutherford has announced an exciting new expedition into the Sonora Desert. The caravan will be embarking on their mission in two days' time and will consist of the Lady herself, Sheriff Sydney Fly of Dead Horse, Arizona, their guide, and several laborers. Lady Ann is the esteemed daughter of...' well, it goes on a bit about her parentage. Those Brits are quite proud of their pedigrees, aren't they?"

"Hey," Adam warned. "Bloody watch it, mate."

William laughed and held up his hands playfully in surrender. "Merely an observation. Then again, thou art the esteemed descendant of the good Robin of Locksley, aye?" William pronounced it all with a terrible British accent. "Stealing from the rich and giving to the poor. Or is it stealing from the rich *and* the poor?"

Shrugging, Adam sauntered over and turned William's ledger around, glancing over the numbers. "Moving zeroes again? I'm in good company, it seems."

"You got me, officer," said William, offering his wrists. "Am I under arrest?"

For the past five years, William had been doing what he colloquially called "moving zeroes." It was hardly a crime, because

Worthington was richer than God, and the man himself had no idea what his net worth really was. Between the two of them, William and Adam had a tidy little sum buried away under the floorboards of their caravan. "How much?"

"Just under nine thousand."

Adam whistled. "Why the hell am I doing this job?"

"Investment capital." William licked the back of his teeth with his tongue, something he only did when his greed had been excited. "If you want that head of cattle we're talking about, you need capital."

For years they had talked about it. The homestead. The cattle. A brand new life far away from men of the likes of Worthington. The only thing Adam didn't get was why they needed so much bloody coin to run a small ranch in the Arizona foothills. He started saying something to that effect, but William cut him off.

"Why not let me worry about our finances?" He snapped the ledger closed. "You do your job, Robin of Locksley. Make the boss happy. Keeps the gears well-oiled, eh?" William gestured in a grand way that encompassed all their plans together. They were not large plans, but they were detailed. "It won't be long now. One more job and we're done, and to hell with Worthington. To hell with them all."

"You better be right, darling," Adam said, leaning down to wrap an arm around William's neck and kiss him on the lips. "You know how much I hate the bloody desert."

Song of the Sonora

The deadpan of the Sonora stretched out before them—brown, flat, desolate. Endless. The dusty winds of Santa Ana blew like distant war horns between the buttes and spewed continuous funnels of sand onto the travelers as they moved slowly through the landscape of thin, twiggy trees and scrub.

Hours earlier, when the caravan first mounted their horses and left Dead Horse, Anna had found it beautiful, even seductive, and as alien in appearance as another world. It looked like something Mr. H.G. Wells might write about. She wondered if all the American explorers and scouts felt this quiver of excitement, this yearning to know and understand their world. To become more a part of it all. She'd thought she could never take in enough of the colorful mesas and buttes, or the queerly flowering, crooked little trees that dotted the landscape. Even the snakes and insects looked beautiful to her, like glinting jewels sparkling across the desert floor.

But now she was discovering that she was growing tired of it. The landscape was redundant, to say the least. Each long mile felt like the last. The gravelly hills rolled on and on, making the horses stumble. The wind was an ear-piercing howl that never let up. Her parasol was doing little to keep the killing sun at bay, and already the skin of her face felt hot and tight. The dry air was making her lungs hurt, and sand was getting into the most unmentionable of places.

As her horse stumble-walked over yet another sandy hillock, Sydney Fly trotted up to her on his paint and grabbed her reins, straightening her pace. He rode easily, as though he'd been born in the saddle, as though he could sit there for hours, even days, without needing a break, whereas Anna could already feel her tailbone aching.

"Holding up?" he asked her.

"Yes, thank you, Mr. Syd." She urged her horse on and stared straight ahead, though her one hand was playing nervously over the silver bracelet on her opposite wrist. What would she find when they reached the oasis? More to the point, would they ever arrive there? They'd been riding almost half a day, and nothing looked any different.

Syd nodded to her. "I noticed you touching that bracelet back in Tacoma's hut."

"Was I? Edmond gave it to me," Anna answered simply. "For my birthday. I gave him a silver pocket watch in return."

"You were close."

"We were. Once."

"What happened?"

Anna swallowed against her parched throat. "He left. He disappointed my father, and they didn't get on after that." She didn't add anything to that. Syd, for all his obvious worldliness, wouldn't understand. No one did.

A half an hour later, Tacoma pulled his horse up alongside them and pointed off in the distance where Anna could see a single sprawling acacia struggling to eke out a living among the stones and sand. "There's an oasis ahead. I suggest we make camp for the night."

"Already?" Anna said. "The sun is still up."

"You'll be surprised by what's involved in setting up," Syd explained. "If we wait until nightfall, we'll be making camp in the dark."

"Oh," Anna said, feeling naïve. It was just another reminder that she was helplessly out of her element. It was all suddenly so real, all of this. This journey of hers. For the hundredth time that day, she wondered if she had made the right decision.

Syd nodded with sympathy. "Don't worry. You'll learn." To Tacoma, he said, "Lead on, my friend."

Anna had underestimated the desert. Though broiling hot during the day, the moment the sun went down, the temperatures plummeted to just above freezing. They spent the next two hours building fires and constructing a simple lean-to out of sticks, shrubs, and ox-hide. Even so, she couldn't bundle up enough or sit close enough to the fire. A chill seemed permanently installed in her bones.

Tacoma disappeared into the desert to meditate, and the other men they had brought with them—a trio of unscrupulous-looking laborers that Sydney hired up in Dead Horse—sat in their own little circle under the acacia, playing cards, drinking whiskey, and making whispery comments she feared might be about her.

Anna un-sheeted Archie's cage and spent some time feeding him bits of jerky and hard tack while Syd fed the fire logs and brush. "You may join your friends, if you like, Mr. Syd," she offered. "I'm quite capable of handling the duties of the fire."

"You've camped?" His mustache twitched with his smile while he plucked out a pipe and went about the business of filling it with crumpled tobacco leaves from his sack.

"Many times, in fact." It was a blatant lie, but a sin she was willing to commit, under the circumstances. Up until her journey to America, Anna had not had much occasion to live rough, but to say that would only make her look snobbish in Syd's eyes. A spoiled child. And perhaps she was, but that was not something she was willing to advertise. Why she was worried about such things, she didn't know.

No, she knew. He would think her a weak female with a fragile constitution. Others had told her that her whole life. Always a slight child, Anna had been born with weak, asthmatic lungs. They hadn't said as much, but she knew that Father and the doctors had fully expected her to expire long before her tenth birthday. Somehow, though, she had survived.

During that time, however, she had spent so much time abed that she'd almost lost the ability to walk. She often found herself bitterly jealous of Edmond's freedom. He could swim and ride horses with all of his friends, whereas Anna could only watch from her window or read about such adventures in her beloved books. Her mother's coddling, her father's constant warnings about her health…it made her insanely angry. Now, she was in the colonies, and no one knew about such things. No one knew her as anything but the robust young woman she was at present.

She couldn't bear to have Syd treat her like some wilting violet, even if the riding was hard on her body or the dry desert air difficult for her damaged lungs to endure. No, she wanted—needed—to face these men toe to toe. She had to.

It was perhaps the only way she would survive this, she thought, glancing over at the scouts giving her a wicked side-eye.

The bedroll was hard, the ground rocky, but she considered this nothing more than a continued challenge as she lay down and folded her arms under her head and stared up at the scattered con-stellations. Discomfort was good, she reflected. It would keep her from becoming too comfortable and letting her guard down.

Before she turned over, she slipped the gun/sword she'd been hiding in her coat all day into the bedroll with her, grabbed Archie's cage, and drew it close to her. She knew he would let her know if anything untoward happened in the night. After that, she tried to sleep with one eye open.

| 8 |

Breathless

The next day brought with it more desert and more uncomfortable riding. Within hours, Anna was aching all over and coughing so hard into a handkerchief that Syd noticed. Her father's multiple warnings came flooding back to her. She could easily push her body too far. She could collapse and die.

"I'll die if I stay here…if I never see Edmond again," she told herself the day she boarded the ship to America. She'd thought that was a very brave and clever thing to say despite being scared half to death, but now she wasn't so sure of herself.

At one point, around noon, a snake spooked one of the pack mules, which managed to shake off some of their supplies before running off between the dunes and disappearing over a rocky crest. Syd laid chase on his paint but returned three-quarters of an hour later, sans mule.

Anna shielded her eyes against the blinding, headachy glare of the sun. Sand was blowing into her eyes, and her hair was full of it. She had tied a bandana around her mouth to keep from swallowing down half the desert.

"Are we going after it?" she mumbled through the dirty cloth.

Syd shook his head. "Not worth it. That damned mule is halfway to Santa Fe by now."

She didn't want to panic, but…

"Syd, that animal had half of our water!"

Syd turned to Tacoma, who shook his old, hoary head. "We'll find water at the next oasis."

But they didn't. They camped under some willow bushes—even the trees had ceased to live here, in one of the harshest environments on earth—and the watering hole that Tacoma remembered from past journeys had dried up, leaving a damp, muddy pit behind. Syd and the men tried to dig a seep hole, but only a handful of brown water managed to bubble up.

That night, Anna unrolled the maps she had brought with her and pinned them to the ground with stones. She moved the lantern closer. They were a little more than sixty miles out from Dead Horse. According to Tacoma, they had to go at least twice that to get to Blood Valley—or, where he believed Blood Valley was located. He had finally admitted that he had never been there and had never known anyone who'd reached it; he was working strictly off the old legends of his people. She decided they could do it if they went on strict rations. Problem was, she wasn't sure the men would listen to her.

Syd wandered over and crouched down, the pipe in his teeth.

Anna coughed into her handkerchief.

"Miss Anna?"

"I'm fine," she lied. She kept searching her handkerchief for telltale signs of sputum and was relieved to see nothing of the sort. "I think I've swallowed some sand."

"That happens."

To change the subject, she shared her concerns about their rations.

He stood up, quiet and stoic, rubbing his chin. His face was bathed in the lantern light so he looked like he was suffering the flames of hell. She had noticed that he seldom showed any expression. Anna frequently found it difficult to tell what he was thinking. Again, she was struck by his ruggedly handsome face and striking blue eyes. Even coated in dust, he was quite dashing, reminding her of heroes in the books of romance she had grown up reading.

A Mr. Darcy in spurs, she thought, and had to look away, lest he see her blush like some silly schoolgirl.

After a moment, he nodded once. "I'll talk to the men."

"But will they listen to you?"

Syd never missed a beat. Kicking at the dirt, he stated, "They'll listen."

The following day, they managed to cover more ground than Anna expected. The men also seemed quieter and more reserved. She wondered what Syd had said to them. Overall, it was a good day, but by nightfall, Anna was starting to worry again. They still had three days' journey ahead of them, and their water bags were running perilously low. Tacoma had not been able to find any of the watering holes he remembered. For the first time, Anna seriously considered turning back. But that would be even more foolish, she told herself. There was no way they were going to be able to cover five or six days of desert with almost no water. They would need to keep going.

At least the men were no longer a threat. That night, as she and Syd nibbled hard tack and sat around the fire, Anna said, "Whatever you said to the men...thank you, Sheriff."

Syd shrugged. "If they can't behave like gentlemen, then they have no business being on this expedition."

Despite her overall exhaustion, she slept uneasily that night. She dreamed about Edmond. Bleary pastiches of her time growing up with him on their father's estate had become *de rigueur* by now, mundane things like the forts they had built, the soldier games they had played, the friends they had had. But tonight, she dreamed about Edmond crossing the desert, alone and parched, at his wit's end as fear and dehydration ate their way through him. His face was drawn and sunburned, his blond hair bleached almost white by the deadly sun. She dreamed of Edmond collapsing in the sand and raising his dying hand to the sky, calling out to her.

She woke with a start when she realized that someone really was screaming. It took her a moment to realize it was Archie. He was leaping frantically around his cage, squealing and chittering with fear.

"Archie!" she cried, grabbing his birdcage and dragging it close while staring blearily around at her surroundings.

There was far too much light and chaos. She could hear the horses screaming. Scrambling out of her bedroll, Anna smelled the smoke for the first time. The campgrounds were on fire, and the horses, tied to some nearby shrubs, were in a mad panic.

"Syd!" she screamed as she bolted straightaway for the horses to untie them, Archie's cage swinging from her hand. "Syd, where are you...?"

A gunshot made her stop dead in her tracks. She realized that strange men on horseback were circling their camp and firing at the horses. *Deliberately trying to scare them off!* Taking a deep breath for courage, Anna liberated the gun/sword from her coat and surged forward...right into the path of a strange man on horseback.

She sidestepped to keep from being run over, and the horse kicked sand in her face as it turned sharply to follow her motion. The man atop it was handsome, bespeckled, and rather posh-looking for having crossed the desert, but there was a cruel slant to his lips, and shadows lurked behind his dark brown eyes.

"Blimey, you're a lively chit, ain'tcha?" he said in a clipped Cockney accent and reached down for her, snagging her wrist in his hand.

Anna shouted and twisted, trying to get him to let her go, but his grip was like steel. Archie's cage flew off into the dark and rolled across the sand. Her bracelet slipped off and the man's greedy smile grew.

"Lovely," he said, sliding Edmond's birthday bracelet under his coat. "You've just had the honor of being pilfered by Bootleg Adam Bell, the direct descendant of Robin of Locksley!"

"Give that back, you bloody barbarian!" Boiling with rage, Anna threw herself at the man named Adam Bell, clinging to his saddle, which had the unexpected effect of unhorsing him.

With a cry, Bootleg Adam Bell fell into the dust. Down off his mount, he wasn't so imposing. Barely taller than she was, she was on him in seconds, lashing out with everything she had. How dare he come into their camp? How dare he take Edmond's bracelet? She punched him square in the eye and he *oofed* from the impact, a satisfying sound.

When she was a child, she had sometimes been bullied by the other children. They had called her a lunger and "dead-girl-walking." As a result, she had studied different forms of self-defense. She had taught herself to punch and kick according to the illustrations she had seen in magazines and books.

Adam Bell swore at her impacts, and his whole body jarred with each punch. He coughed out an expletive so vile, she stood up and kicked him in the side, making him scream. She then dug her bracelet out of his inside pocket, slid it on, and, with a cry, she gave him one last swift kick in the side.

His whole body jumped. Robin of Locksley, indeed! He looked like he was about to say something, maybe beg for mercy, when another horseman headed her way. She recognized him as one of Worthington's Rough Riders...and he was riding straight for her. She grabbed up her gun/sword...aimed it...

...and was roughly grabbed out of the way. Seconds later, she was tumbling over the sand dunes with Syd wrapped about her. She screeched and fought. Syd swore under his breath as they rolled to a stop perilously close to a cluster of cacti.

"Hell, woman...!" he swore, sitting up.

"Let me go! Release me immediately!"

"I don't think so," Syd said, struggling to his feet with Anna in his grip and pressed flush to his chest. She twisted and fought, the weapon in her hand, so Syd grabbed it away from her.

"Jesus, woman! What the hell do you think you're doing?"

"Killing those marauders!"

"We're outnumbered! Even if you got one, three more would end you!"

She stopped struggling as Syd set her down, though he kept her gun/sword away from her, she noticed. His logic was infuriating.

"What do we do, then?" She glanced around in a panic. The horses had already run off, and the fire was spreading as the dry vegetation went up all around them. Already their campsite was as bright as noontime. The guides were nowhere to be found, though she spotted Tacoma racing toward them.

"Right now? We get out of here." Syd grabbed her wrist.

She pulled away. "Wait."

Turning, she raced to grab up a sack of supplies and then changed direction suddenly where she spotted Archie's cage fall. All she found was some mangled bamboo lying in the sand. The cage had been completely destroyed, and Archie...Archie was gone. By then, Syd was upon her.

"Archie!" Anna screamed into the night even as Syd dragged her away and the whole camp erupted into flames. *"Archie!"*

2

EXPLORATION

| 9 |

Blood Valley

Two days later, Adam was still smarting from the thrashing the little blonde chit had given him. He hadn't expected that. She had looked so slight that he was certain a strong wind could blow her away, but she kicked like a bloody mule! His ribs were purple and bruised, and as his horse climbed yet another hillock, the jostling in the saddle made them scream in protest. As soon as he had topped the rocky dune, he stopped and dismounted, checking his injuries in the little toiletry mirror he'd brought in his rucksack.

His eye was still half-swollen shut, and the bruises along his jawline had only just begun to yellow.

Worthington's Rough Riders gathered about him, all coarse men who had worked in the carnival for years. Some were carnies, but most were outlaws who had attached themselves to Worthington for the same reason as he—protection from the law. Adam liked none of them. They were greedy, hungry, dangerous men. They would cut their own mums' throats for a payday.

Their leader, a man named Bill Clanton, was a former Cowboy who had been in direct conflict with Wyatt, Virgil, and Morgan

Earp. He catcalled to Adam as he dismounted. "No worries, pretty boy, you're still the belle of the ball!"

Adam squinted up at the man in disgust. "Get back on your horse, Clanton."

Clanton stepped up and pushed his hat back. "Not till we know how far. My men are getting cooked under this godforsaken sun."

"We get there when we get there."

But that wasn't good enough for the Rough Riders, who had begun to grumble dangerously. To forestall a mutiny, Adam fished his spyglass out and glassed the desert horizon. He reported, "Fifteen miles as the crow flies."

Clanton spat and kicked the earth. "You shoulda brought that girl. We coulda had a good time with her."

One of Clanton's men laughed. "He couldn't kidnap her, Bill. Pretty boy here was too busy getting his ass kicked by her."

"And ogling the sheriff," another put in.

"Talk about a firecracker," Clanton said with a wide, leering grin. He rubbed his chin as his thoughts turned inward and toward Lady Anna Rutherford. "Warm your cockles, that's for sure."

All the men laughed.

Adam ground his teeth. As much as he had it out for the chit with the mule kick, the last thing he wanted was a woman falling into the hands of these thugs. "No time for girls, Clanton. Tell your boys to get back on their horses. We're riding down to the valley tonight."

"Camp first," Clanton insisted. "Valley at first light."

"Oi! We'll camp when we get there," Adam snapped, losing all patience. He turned and shot Clanton a look. He could look fairly imposing when he had a mind to. But to be on the safe side, he pushed his great coat back to reveal his rig. "Now get on yer bloody nags, ye slags!"

Still grumbling, the men reluctantly re-mounted and headed out. Several hours later, sometime in the late afternoon, they saw the valley for the first time with their own eyes. The oasis was larger than Adam had expected, stretching as far as the eye could see to the horizon, a blot of eye-watering green in the middle of the desolate, colorless terrain.

In his travels with Worthington's show, Adam had seen oases before in the desert, of course, but never this large. It looked like a whole different world made of frothy green ferns and strange, coniferous trees rearing up in the distance as if it had been cut out of the earth half a world away and transported here. A huge waterway cut through the valley, bisecting the oasis. Ostentatiously, this was the source of the verdant life. The river seemed to emerge magically from the desert floor and sliced a silvery swath through the wild flora of the valley before disappearing behind hills of jungle green.

After walking in the scorchingly dry desert for days and living off hot, rationed water, Adam could smell the cool river and living trees. They pulled on him like a magnet. There was even a pleasant breeze that smelled of fresh water, and it was one of the most seductive things he had ever experienced.

"Blood Valley," Adam said, halting his horse and studying it. For a long moment, he let his eyes and brain take in all that delicious green. It was paradise after days of seeing the same bland desert colors. He wasn't certain why it seemed to have such an intimidating reputation. As far as he was concerned, this was nirvana. This was salvation. The desert around them was nothing but death.

The Rough Riders' horses whickered and shifted side to side; they, too, smelled fresh water. Whether it was the riders' intentions or not, they started cantering down the steep incline toward the oasis, drawn as he was to the greenness of the valley far below. Adam followed behind a little more hesitantly. He started to tell them to slow down, but then found himself trotting along behind them as his thirsty horse hurried to keep up with the others. A cloud of dust followed them as they closed in on Blood Valley.

After another hour of hard riding, they reached the foothills of the oasis for the first time and looked upon a land that only a handful of Navajo Braves had ever seen—and fewer still had ever walked away from. Unsurprisingly, there were a number of un-marked graves set into the foothills, mostly burial cairns and small megaliths, the desert being too dry to dig too deeply. Adam felt a shiver down his back as he reined his horse in and reached for his canteen, which was nearly dry. He could only assume these were the poor, lost bastards who hadn't survived the desert. Some of the cairns bore crudely scratched names on the headstones, all Anglo-Saxon. Worthington's last expedition, he reckoned, led by that fool, Edmond Rutherford, though he didn't see Rutherford's name on any of the graves.

He was sipping the last, retchingly hot remnants of his water and wondering if Rutherford had somehow managed to survive living in the valley this past year when he heard one of his men shout a warning. A gunshot went off, and another man yodeled in fear.

"Hell," he said, and kicked his horse into a canter.

Something was crashing through the trees up ahead. It sounded like a stampede of horses, though it bellowed like a gigantic, angry bull. As Adam cleared the tree line and topped a rocky ridge, he saw it for the first time.

It was the size of a young bull elephant, compact and powerful, and armed with a frilly, head, beaked jaws, and a single, curved nasal horn as large as a man rising from its snout. Its shiny black eyes were tiny and terror-filled as the Rough Riders surrounded it. It lowed and fought, caught up in several of the Rough Riders' ropes, which it was pulling like a mad bull at.

The men hooted and hollered, surrounding and distracting the beast. It thrashed its formidable head from side to side and clacked its jaws together, making a series of short, harsh, almost bird-like calls of distress, but the Rough Riders were a fearless bunch of dumb thugs, if they were nothing else. Though the creature was surely strong enough to move a locomotive off its tracks, it was no match for the group of men on horseback, many of whom were former Cowboys, and some of whom had been rustling cattle since before Adam was born.

Worthington's orders had been clear enough. Adam's prerogative was twofold: to track the Rutherford Expedition, upset it by any means necessary, and use the map that his boss had given him to reach Blood Valley. From there, they were to capture as many specimens alive as they could. But the ways things were going, Adam wasn't sure if the men gave a good goddamn about that last part.

He swore under his breath as the Riders brought the animal crashing to its knees. It trumpeted long and hard, scattering a flock of strange-looking birds from the trees overhead. Clanton, who had been directing the whole operation, broke away from the other man and galloped up to Adam, a greedy smile cutting across the black desert grime on his face. He hooked a thumb back over his shoulder. "Whatta ya think, pretty boy? Quite the beaut."

"I think we were supposed to set up camp," Adam said, sounding angrier than he should have. He didn't know why, but the man was rankling him in an awful way. It was the desert, he decided. Bloody desert. The ranch and William had better be worth all this grief. It wasn't hell, exactly, but he could see it from where he stood.

"Think Worthington will give us a bonus?"

"I think he'll kick your teeth out if you kill that animal."

Clanton shrugged, showing off his broken brown grin. "If it croaks, we'll just find another one. There's a whole herd of these bastards back there!" he said, nodding toward the jungle before turning his horse around and trotting back to where the men were pegging the ropes to the ground, the creature trussed up beneath and bellowing miserably.

"Bloody tosser." If Adam had this way, he'd have shot half of Worthington's men.

A short time later, he heard the crunch of vegetation somewhere to the east. He turned and dug out the pince-nez and examined the surrounding jungle. The X-ray glasses cut through the foliage like a hot knife through butter, and it wasn't long before he spotted the bulk of the creature heading their way.

"Shit…" he started, and tried to give warning, but his voice was cut off by the cries of the men as a creature similar to the one they had captured, only larger, lunged out of the underbrush. Though it was gigantic, it moved with liquid grace, barely rattling the leaves on the trees. It shook its frilly head and ten-foot nasal horn, and, with a mighty bellow of pure, unadulterated rage, charged them all.

| 10 |

Welcome to the Jungle

C oughing, Anna dropped to her knees on the scorching desert floor. A series of hacking coughs wracked her body for several minutes.

Syd suddenly appeared beside her. "Anna…"

She held up a hand and took a few deep, rattling breaths before clearing her throat. "I'm all right, Sheriff. Truly. A bit of dust."

She climbed to her feet, nearly stumbling. Syd took her by the elbow to steady her on her quivery legs. For once, she didn't slap away his hand or complain about his chivalrous gestures. After walking in the desert for two days with no water, no food, no horses, and the sun pulsing down overhead, slowly baking her to death, she was almost to the point of giving up, giving in.

She now lived every moment of her life exhausted and on the very knife-edge of tears. The desert was hell, plain and simple. It did not love her. It did not love anyone, and it was slowly eating away all of her pride. Edmond was missing. Archie was gone. They were going to die—she, Syd and Mr. Tacoma—and it was all her fault.

Hers. She had dragged them out here, and she was going to be the death of them all.

"I'm sorry," Syd said. His hand on her arm was all that kept her on her feet at the moment. "About your bird."

"Archie…yes. I'm sorry, too," she began, her voice an almost airless gasp out of her dry, parched throat. She wanted to cry—needed to cry—but she was so dry, she didn't even have the tears. The desert had taken even that from her.

Straightening up, she decided to tell the whole truth. "Syd, I think I may have made a terrible mist—"

Her words were interrupted by Tacoma's cry. He was perched atop a rise, his hands cupped around his mouth as he shouted something in Navajo to Syd.

Syd raised a hand to shield his eyes from the relentless sun, but his face was transformed by the news. Despite the sand in his mustache, he looked positively radiant. "An oasis," Syd said, turning to Anna. He took her hand in his large, rough one. "Tacoma says he spots water."

"What…?" Anna said, shocked to the very dregs of her soul.

"Water," Syd repeated, translating the Navajo for Anna. "And some kind of giant oasis."

Water. The oasis.

Blood Valley.

Despite the losses, the exhaustion…despite everything…they had made it. They had made it!

Anna smiled, laughed, then promptly passed out from pure exhaustion.

* * *

"Anna?" the voice called out. "Anna, is it you, darling?"

It was Edmond's voice.

Anna opened her eyes and sat up. It was full dark out and she was alone in the desert, the sky all black velvet and full of light. It was cooler now, almost uncomfortably so. Her head spun, but somehow she managed to scramble up.

"Edmond?" she called, finding her footing. "Edmond, where are you?"

"Anna? Anna, can you hear me?" the voice whispered out of the almost impenetrable dark. "Can you save me?"

Anna spun in a circle. "Edmond, where are you?"

"Here, Anna! I'm here!"

The voice seemed to come from only one direction, but in the dark, it was hard to tell which direction that was. Dusting herself off, Anna hurried toward where she thought the voice was loudest. She didn't get very far, however. The sand here was so soft that every footfall seemed to make her sink deeper and deeper. Within minutes, she was knee deep and plowing through the darkness with every inch of her strength. Still, she kept calling out to Edmond, trying to find him by the sound of his voice.

"Edmond...? *Edmond!*"

Her brother cried out as if in pain. The sound zipped up her back like a razor blade.

"Edmond!" she cried in response. "I'm coming!" She tried to scramble forward, but the sand of the Sonora sucked her down and down. Before long, she was up to her waist, then her shoulders. Anna threw her arms out at the darkness and screamed...

* * *

Anna jerked awake.

At first, she thought she was still sinking into the soft sand in her dream. It took her a moment to realize someone was holding her down. "No!"

"Anna, take it easy! You're having a nightmare." Syd. Syd was holding her down, trying to keep her from flailing around and hurting herself. She gasped and her limbs trembled and went limp.

Only then did he let her go and lean back away from her. "Anna...are you awake?"

She rubbed her aching head. Feeling groggy, like she was emerging from a long-term illness, Anna pushed herself into a sitting position, using the wall of rock at her back for support. "I...I think so. What happened?"

Again she touched her head. She had an ugly, throbbing bump on her forehead.

Syd looked at her with concern. He was holding what seemed like a full canteen of water in one hand, which he was rattling. Droplets of water rolled down its side, making the saliva pool in her parched mouth. "You fell and hit your head pretty hard. Tacoma and I thought you'd killed yourself, woman. Here."

He handed her the full canteen.

She swallowed down greedy mouthfuls of water while he explained how he had carried her the last quarter mile to this place. The water was cold and fresh. Anna drank down half the canteen before choking on the water and coming up for breath.

"Oh," she said, the cold water giving her a pulsing headache. "How long was I out?" "A few hours," Syd told her. "Not long."

Her thirst sated, she glanced around her surroundings. In her dreams, she had still been lost deep in the desert, calling out for Edmond, but here the desert had given way to greener, lush terrain. The acacia trees and scrubby bushes had returned, and just over the next ridge, she could see the top of some kind of tall, coniferous tree.

Trees. Just beyond the rocky outcropping where they were camped was a stand of trees. Anna scrambled to her feet and took a few unsteady steps, shielding her eyes from the fierceness of the setting sun. Syd offered her his hand, and despite her pride, she took it and let him help her climb the ridge on her watery legs.

Together, they stood at the top. Below her lay the whole of Blood Valley, a froth of verdant green with the silver ribbon of a river running through it. Tall, strange-looking coniferous trees stretched away as far as the eye could see, with birds similar to Archie dancing through their branches and chasing giant dragonflies.

"The valley..." she said, breathing out. She turned to Syd. "Blood Valley. Syd, we made it."

Without giving it much thought, she tilted her head skyward and screamed like a madwoman, "We made it!" She then threw herself at him as her heart filled with hope for the first time in what seemed like forever.

Syd caught her easily, actually laughing as he struggled to support her weight around his neck, something she figured would have been no problem for him had he had something more in the way of sustenance than a few sips of water and a few bites of jerky over the last few days. As it was, they both fell down, laughing, while Tacoma looked on with curiosity.

Anna didn't care. "Look!" she cheered, pointing upward at the nearest coniferous tree. She recognized the unique pattern of the bird. Sitting in the uppermost branches was Archie, twittering with excitement and looking down expectantly on them both.

| **11** |

Death from the Sky

By first light, they were packed and ready to head down the sharp incline to the edge of the valley. Water from a nearby spring and a roasted lizard that Syd had managed to scare up out of a hole was all that was fortifying them at this point, but, somehow, it was enough.

"What do you think, Archie?" Anna asked, feeding him the last bit of hard tack from her pack. He perched in the crook of her elbow, scarfing down the last crumbs. He was acting as if no time had passed since his release. "Do you want to go with us?"

Tacoma eyed her skeptically from beneath the brim of his hat. "You said you would let the Old One go." He slung his pack over one slightly stooped shoulder.

"I've been trying, Mr. Tacoma. He just won't fly away!" Anna explained.

She raised her arm to show. Archie would flutter up, then settle on her arm once more and wait for more treats. In truth, she hoped he wouldn't go. She had gotten rather attached to him.

Syd put a hand on the old man's shoulder. "The Old One has chosen her. You aren't going to argue with an Old One, are you, my friend?"

Tacoma shrugged in response as they started down the ridge.

Anna started out at a brisk walk, but it wasn't long before she had hitched up her skirts and was running full tilt toward the line of trees up ahead, Archie gliding smoothly behind her, but never very far off. She stumbled twice but did not fall. Breathless and almost on the verge of collapse, she reached the tree line, charged into the jungle, and headed for the first pool of water she saw. She only slowed as she reached the water's edge.

Once she arrived, she dropped her pack and waded in, boots and all, as Syd appeared behind her, followed by Tacoma. Tacoma was muttering something in Navajo. He did not sound pleased, and his eyes kept darting all around the jungle.

Anna ignored the old man. Standing knee-deep in the water, she splashed cold water on her face and over her long, tangled hair before standing up and spinning in a circle.

"Edmond! I'm here! I'm here for you!" she called, hoping against hope that he would call back.

Nothing.

The only sound she heard was the bizarre, nasally bird-like sounds in the jungle, sounds she had never heard before, and Archie whistling as he circled overhead.

"Ed—" she began anew, but Syd suddenly appeared behind her and put a hand over her mouth. She mumbled, turning sharply in his embrace to give him what for...then saw him pointing toward the water they were standing in.

"Look," he said quietly in her ear.

Bubbles were forming on the surface of the pond. Anna's eyes widened at the sight and she felt something like a giant fist squeezing her heart in a panic. A moment later, a dead man bounced to the surface, mangled and broken, and that was it. Anna screamed from behind Syd's hand.

* * *

"Trampled," Syd said, crouching over the body of what Anna could only guess was once a Rough Rider. It was hard to tell. There wasn't very much left of the man. He looked like a bag of loose bones and tattered flesh and clothes. Syd used his booted foot to kick the body onto its back. "Yep…trampled. I've seen enough horse stampedes to know."

"Trampled," Anna said, standing over the man. The sight of him made her nauseous, but she refused to look away. She told herself she was tougher than that. "This doesn't look like any trampling I've ever seen."

"It was big, whatever it was," Syd responded. "The size of an elephant. Maybe larger."

Something caught Anna's attention. Over Syd's shoulder, she could see birds circling like kites, riding the hot updrafts off the desert. They were huge, and, unlike Archie, nearly featherless. They looked more like bats than birds. Occasionally, they flapped their stiff wings and screamed, their cries bouncing off the stone walls of the valley and vibrating through the still air.

Tacoma noticed. as well, and pointed. "The dragons have come."

"Dragons," Syd said, reaching for the colt on his hip while Tacoma set his booted foot against a young stripling and broke it off at the base for a spear, but somehow Anna didn't think one puny little gun and a stick was going to be enough to fend off those creatures.

"Those aren't dragons. They're pteranodon," Anna explained. "A pterosaur that lived during the late Cretaceous Period. I wrote a thesis on them, once."

"So they're dinosaurs," said Syd with some awe.

"Technically, no. They don't belong to the order *Dinosauria*. Rather, they're a predecessor to modern birds."

"Well, whatever they are, they look hungry."

Anna had managed to salvage the gun/sword from their camp when the Rough Riders had set it ablaze and had tied it to her waist with a scarf. She pulled it free now, but she still felt terribly insignificant in the face of the giant birds circling what looked like some kind of giant rookery dug out of a giant volcanic crater. Young and almost naked birds clung to the walls, with nests full of eggs on top of the shelf.

She thought it was possible the ones in the air were being drawn to the scent of the dead man at their feet. "They're scavengers. Opportunistic hunters," she muttered more to herself than anyone else. "Isn't that interesting? I shall have to write a new thesis..."

They drifted up and up in the air like kites, then swooped down, only to repeat the maneuver. Each time they did, they drew just a little bit closer to the trio. It didn't take long for Anna to figure out what they were doing.

"Syd..." she warned, but was interrupted when one broke off from the flock, changed trajectory with shocking speed, and headed straight for them. "Syd!"

The pteranodon reached them in seconds—in no more time than the it took between one breath and the next. It screamed hysterically and clacked its huge, cone-like beak at them.

Tacoma, standing behind them, was faster than either of them. He stabbed at the pterosaur with his impromptu spear. The creature shrieked, snapping its jaws wildly, the spear protruding from one eye. Syd swore and aimed his colt at the struggling bird, but before he could squeeze off a shot, another pterosaur swept by, shrieking and nearly deafening Anna, the wind from its wings knocking her to her face on the ground.

Shrieking in response, she flipped over onto her back to better follow it, but it was too fast. Making another pass, it caught Syd's long cowboy coat in its claws. It wasn't as large as the first bird—maybe the size of a mule—but it had strength enough to lift Syd right off his feet and drag him up into the air, where a panicked Archie was swooping and twittering with frenzied fear.

Syd yelped in response and tried to lift his gun arm, but he was badly off-balance and his shot went wild. The pteranodon jiggled him in mid-air and Syd dropped his colt, which disappeared into some vegetation.

"Syd!" Anna screamed, bolting to her feet. She raced forward, her gun/sword at the ready, but the way the creature hovered with Syd twisting and pedaling uselessly in the air, it was impossible for her to properly scope the bird and not hit Syd.

Archie circled the creature's head, snapping and hissing for everything he was worth. The pteranodon clacked its beak at the little bird, but Archie was too quick for it and easily evaded the other bird. Finally, the creature made a low, angry warbling sound in its throat and shot off into the jungle...with Syd still clutched in its talons.

| 12 |

Follow That Bird

Her heart thundering like war drums, Anna ran on and on, Tacoma at her heels. The jungle blurred into a vague green hell around them. The limbs of the strangely stunted coniferous trees thwacked them in the faces as they raced blindly in the direction of the giant bird. The ground went from dry and solid to damp and fecund, full of pine-like needles. The vegetation was changing, but Anna noticed this only peripherally. She couldn't risk losing sight of the pteranodon carrying her friend off into the jungle.

Thankfully, Syd was a large man, and certainly no flyweight. The pteranodon, despite its great size, flew awkwardly in an odd zig-zagging pattern and was unable to clear the treetops whilst carrying his weight. Still, keeping up with the bird was taking everything out of her, and within minutes, Anna started to wheeze and her chest felt like there was a boulder on it.

Now, there was less desert brush and small trees and more flowering jungle—larger trees full of vines and wildly growing, frilly flowers that were gigantic and full of color. Any other time, and she might have been able to appreciate their strange, primeval beauty. Right now, though, Anna's legs were pounding tirelessly like pistons against the ground as she pushed herself on and on. Syd, meanwhile, was being jerked this way and that by the huge bird as it fumbled through the trees. He looked like a rag doll being carried away, and Anna could only imagine his terror.

Ahead, she spotted the cliffs across the vast ravine that acted as the pteranodons' rookery. The other birds were roosting, many upside down against the sides of the cliffs. And then, of course, there were the nests full of squalling young.

"Dear God!" Anna exclaimed, skidding to a stop. Tacoma, who, despite his age, had been keeping pace with her with no problem, also stopped.

"Miss!" He pointed at the birds. "They are taking him."

"Not if I can help it," she said and hefted the gun/sword up, leveling it against her forearm and resting the stock against her shoulder. Her breath shuddered as she took a bead on the bird, trying not to hurry. If she hurried...if her shot went wild...Syd was finished.

"Miss, it's getting away!"

"Yes, I see," she said, her voice eerily calm. She caressed the trigger, almost squeezed it, then stopped to take another deep breath and resettle the gun. By now, the bird was almost to the edge of the drop-off. She had seconds, if that, before the bird was too far for her to get an accurate shot.

Saying a soft prayer, Anna squeezed the trigger.

* * *

The bird was dead. It took the combined strength of Anna and Tacoma to push it off Syd, who was lying beneath.

"Uhh," he said, sounding breathless and broken. He had landed in some ferns, which at least helped to break his fall, but the bird that had landed atop him wasn't helping in the least.

"Syd? Syd, are you all right?" Anna knelt down to check on him. She ran a hand over his legs. "Anything broken?"

"Don't think so," Syd responded, coughing. He struggled into a sitting position, then let loose a string of curses that left Anna blushing like a virgin on her wedding night.

"Help me with him!" Tacoma insisted, and he and Anna each took an arm, slung it across their shoulders, and hauled Syd to his almost six-and-a-half-foot height, not without great effort on each of their parts. He limped as Anna handed him back his colt, which she at least had had the presence of mind to retrieve before their impromptu little run through the jungle. Overall, he looked scuffed up but appeared to be all right. She thought it was possible that only his pride had been broken.

"At least we have meat now," Tacoma said, prodding the dead bird with his boot, but Anna didn't answer.

She was too busy pawing through some underbrush, trying to find a branch that would make a decent crutch for Syd to lean on. She'd thought she'd found one when something that sounded like thunder seemed to roll across the sky.

"Now what?" she asked no one in particular, looking upward. "Is there a storm coming?"

Syd limped to her side, listening. "I don't think so." He took her hand, which didn't reassure her in the least. He turned to the sound. So did Tacoma, who had been busy constructing a new spear.

Seconds later, Syd's bright blue eyes grew wide at the sight before them. "Run!"

***

Anna thought about the trampled man they had found in the pond as the herd of *Centrosaurus* charged them, looking like a collection of angry, runaway locomotives. She knew what they were; she had studied them extensively in literature. There was a pod of at least a dozen of the horned, frilled beasts, maybe more, all of different sizes and, presumably, sexes, but Anna wasn't about to make any further scientific observations about that. They were bellowing, kicking up tons of earth, and flattening trees as they ran full tilt toward the three explorers.

"Dear God..."

"That way," Tacoma said, pointing toward a cave entrance carved into a prehistoric mountain. It was just visible through a clearing about a quarter of a mile away. If they could get to it, the large animals wouldn't be able to follow. The question was whether they could cross the distance before the pod reached them.

Even though all three were exhausted, they ran like their lives, quite literally, depended on it, past the strange, stunted trees, and the huge, flowering jungle vegetation, past muddy sinkholes and huge pod-like plants with strangely sentient vines coiling along the jungle floor like snakes. One tripped Anna up and she nearly fell, only to be saved by Syd and Tacoma as each grabbed her by an arm, urging her on, faster and faster.

It wasn't long before her legs felt weak and she was nearly out of breath. Her heart felt like it was going to burst right through her ribs. And still she ran. Behind them rolled the angry wave of death —animals that had likely been enraged by their encounter with the Rough Riders, their first experience with white men. The Rough Riders had taught the pod cruelty, violence, and distrust, and now cruelty, violence, and distrust was their way.

They had almost reached the edge of the clearing when a pair of new creatures lunged out of nowhere—and right into their path. These were different than the pod behind them, tall, upright creatures with huge, swinging heads full of hook-like, predatory teeth and two protruding horns above their eyes, giving them a disgruntled, bull-like appearance.

Anna recognized them immediately from her studies and stuck her heels in, lurching to a halt and pulling her two companions to a stop beside her. All three of them stared up at the enormous creatures stalking toward them. Anna blurted out a curse that she had heard Syd use.

"*Carnotaurus*," she whispered, edging back a step.

"What?" Syd asked, drawing his gun once more.

Anna raised her gun/sword, for all the good that was likely to do them. "It's their name. *Carnotaurus*. It means 'meat-eating bull.'"

"Well, hell," Syd cursed. "Thank God I know that."

The pair of *Carnotauruses* took one look at them, grunted, and charged.

| **13** |

The Horror at Hooked Rock

Adam stuck his booted foot on the crosspiece of the bow, gritted his teeth, and cranked the crossbow back, priming a bolt from the quiver he carried on his back. He lifted the crossbow to his shoulder, feet shoulders-wide as he balanced at the edge of the pteranodons' rookery.

"Hello there, mate," he said to the giant predatory bird scrambling bat-like across the ground at him. The prehistoric bird had its beak wide open, and it was screaming like a banshee out of hell. His finger caressed the trigger, and he studied the bird for a moment through the sight. Then he turned and fired the bolt into the opposite side of the ravine where the birds were roosting—what he had come to think of as Hooked Rock, due to the way they were hanging upside down like bats.

He felt the shriek of wind beating against his face as the bird sailed over him. He threw himself down, missing it, and watching as the bird flew right into the rope attached to the bolt. The bird screamed as it was flung to the ground, wounded but not mutilated, not like the others that his remaining men had brought down with their guns and their greed.

Crumpled pteranodon bodies littered the ground, including a number of slow, slug-like young who had been clinging to the underside of their parents when the adult birds were felled by Clanton's idiot men. More were dead than were alive.

Yesterday's debacle with the *Centrosauruses* had almost been a disaster. Panicked, the creatures had trampled one of Clanton's gunmen, not that that was any kind of loss, mind you. The men were cowardly idiots, and Adam couldn't wait to be done with the lot of them.

The *Centrosauruses* had proven to be almost more than the men could handle. Huge brutes with a vengeance, the juvenile *Centrosaurus* they had captured had brought the whole herd down upon them like thunder and lighting. It had taken the men all of their munitions just to chase them off, and when it was done, they still had had to deal with what had to have been the juvenile's mother. She refused to leave the juvenile, no matter how many guns they fired in her direction, or how many bullets she took.

The old girl had finally collapsed beside her young, and both had been dutifully added to the Worthington collection.

Another bird flew into his rope and crashed to the ground at his feet. Meanwhile, the men were picking through the fallen birds and tying ropes to those that looked promising, hauling them onto the gigantic litters they had been working on all day long in preparation for the journey back across the desert.

Clanton moseyed over, his rifle resting on his shoulder and a disgusting, blood-splattered grin on his face that Adam wanted to slap off. "Them's two good birds. I think we're done here."

"And how many did you kill to get two good ones?"

Clanton shrugged and then spat in the dirt. "My men are tired."

"I say when we're done here," Adam reminded the man, lifting the bow up so it was resting against his other arm. A part of him wanted to hit Clanton in the face with it, but he figured he might break it that way. Would feel bloody good, though.

His personal fantasy was interrupted when he heard a scream of bloody murder from one of his men. He turned to the sound, the crossbow drooping at his side. "Bloody hell...!"

From the jungle poured a flock of flightless birds taller than men. They had gigantic hooked beaks and piercing screams. They sported blood-red crests high upon their heads, and their eyes were full of murder and a need for blood and meat. Despite their impressive size, they moved slickly, with a predatory grace. The first one snipped the head off one of Clanton's men like a child taking a pair of scissors to her paper doll. The man screamed even as his head was gobbled down the throat of the bird and the rest of him crumpled to the blood-splattered ground. The other Rough Riders just stared at the carnage, and one man was sick on his knees.

Meanwhile, the birds gathered together and surveyed the area, squawking with interest. They did a queer little dance with their heads carried low and crests raised high, scratching and stomping the ground as they took inventory of what had to be a moveable feast to them. Some of the birds leaped upon the wounded pteranodons and began the process of feasting upon the prehistoric avians even before they were fully dead. Others turned their greedy gimlet eyes on the men still alive and breathing.

Most of Adam's men, struck with a kind of terror-filled paralysis, just stood there, gaping at this new horror. Bill Clanton, though, raised his rifle and took aim. "Son of a bitch," he said as he opened fire on the birds.

"I hate this bloody place!" Adam shouted, reaching for another bolt as one of the angry-looking birds zeroed in on him. The other men followed suit, scrambling belatedly for weapons even as the massacre commenced.

Blood and Stone

Syd pushed Anna out of the path of the two charging *Carnotauruses.*

The two of them tumbled in the brush at the edge of the clearing. Tacoma stood his ground, spear in hand, which Anna knew would be of no benefit to him. But it was his stand to make.

It was also his last.

The *Carnotauruses* moved faster than anything Anna had ever seen. They were on him in seconds. Tacoma made a half-hearted attempt to stab at one of the creature's eyes, but they easily evaded the weapon. Seconds later, the mated pair were playing tug of war with his body, ripping him to pieces like a bloody doll. Anna heard someone screaming. She was pretty sure it was she who was doing the screaming, but somehow she couldn't stop herself.

"He...he...he..." she hiccupped.

Syd pulled her up. "He saved us, is what he did."

Just then, the pod of *Centrosauruses* burst from the jungle, grunting and growling. An old bull—likely their leader—took one look at the pair of *Carnotauruses* and decided to take all of his rage and insult out on them. He charged the pair, and the *Carnotauruses* bellowed a warning, but the pod came anyway, rumbling over the hill like a pack of runaway horses. Anna never expected them to be so aggressive, but the Rough Riders had riled them up well and good.

In seconds, the *Carnotauruses* were trapped in the middle of the pod. They snapped at their enemies' horned heads with their giant, slavering jaws while the angry, armored beasts pawed the ground and clacked their beaked mouths in warning, tossing their massive horns at the large predators. The bull lashed out at the larger *Carnotaurus*, and the creature—the Missus, Anna thought—jumped onto its back, biting at the back of his neck. The *Centrosaurus* screamed and tossed his head from side to side while a primeval struggle for life and victory enveloped the two.

"Let's get the hell out of here," Syd said, grabbing Anna's arm and racing with her toward the nearby cave.

* * *

The sounds the warring animals made was making Anna's hair stand on end. The growls. The impacts. The raw, copper penny smell of the blood as they tore savagely into one another. She stumbled around in a daze for a few seconds before collapsing to her knees and throwing up all over the sandy floor of the cave.

Anna had always thought of herself as a strong person, but as she rubbed the sour webbing of sick from her lips with her sleeve, she started having her doubts. She'd thought she was a person who could handle anything. She'd taken the long, arduous journey to the colonies in stride. She hadn't even panicked when she'd initially learned that Edmond was missing. Instead, she had carefully made her plans, calculating everything down to the last detail, as usual.

She hadn't let life in the "Wild West" affect her at all. In fact, she had striven—and succeeded—to keep her composure and pride intact.

But now, suddenly, with Tacoma dead and the beasts savaging each other mere yards away, she felt like she could take no more. She started to cry—great, heaving sobs that left her breathless and gasping—her hands over her face.

Syd hovered near the mouth of the cave, gun drawn for protection but otherwise saying nothing, and for that, she was grateful. He was a good, mostly silent, man, not given to lecturing her about her actions, her thoughts, or her decisions like so many she had known. The last thing she needed was some man hovering over her and berating her while she made a fool of herself. It was bad enough she was breaking down in front of him.

When had her life become this nightmare? Even when her parents were certain she would die and had been prepared to call the vicar, she had not felt this raw-edged terror. This utter, blind, mind-numbing shock. Back then, Edmond had visited her often while she lay in her sick bed. He'd read to her or had done magic tricks to raise her spirits. He had made her laugh when there was very little to laugh about. Where was he now? Where was her Edmond?

"Edmond..." Rolling into a ball on the cold, rocky floor, Anna cried herself to sleep for the first time in years.

| 15 |

After

It was quiet when she woke up. Not silent, but quiet. *Quieter*. The sounds of battle outside the cave had stopped.

As Anna sat up, all she could detect was the twittering of strange insects and the occasional, distant hunting call of some prehistoric animal deep in the jungle.

Syd had started a fire in a stone pit. He sat on the edge of the pit, pushing embers around with a branch. Archie, despite all the violence of the last few hours, had found his way back to them and was perched on one of Syd's strong shoulders, but the moment he realized Anna was awake, he started to chatter with excitement. Syd noticed, too, and said, "It's over. They're gone. I think they all wounded each other."

Anna pushed unruly hair out of her face, rubbed at the multitude of scratches and insect bites on her cheeks. She didn't want to say anything about how she had behaved earlier. She was far too ashamed. And exhausted. She simply got up and crept uneasily to the mouth of the cave. It was almost pitch black out, but a wave of meaty death smell hit her nostrils, tightened her stomach muscles, and almost making her heave again.

Several large, dead animals lay strewn across the ground, rib bones exposed, the meat still steaming in the coolness of the night. She recognized them as *Centrosauruses*. Some looked half-eaten. Others simply looked ripped apart. The battle had not gone well for the rampaging herbivores. Their rage had been their undoing.

Clamping a hand over her mouth, Anna wandered back to the fire and sat down. Archie took the opportunity to glide to her and alight on her shoulder, warbling softly into her hair. She noticed after a moment that Syd had a piece of *Centrosaurus* meat grilling among the coals.

He offered her a sympathetic smile. "Sorry. It's the only thing available."

She shook her head even as she sat there, rubbing her sore stomach. "No worries. I'm not hungry, actually."

Syd prodded at the meat with his stick before reaching down to rip a burned piece off and offer it to Anna. She looked at it with disgust, yet her traitorous stomach rumbled all the same. She couldn't remember the last time she had eaten anything at all, and the juicy meat—as horrible as it was—made the emptiness inside her resound. "Tastes like chicken."

Anna suddenly laughed at that. Her laughter sounded less than sane.

They chewed their meat in silence for a while. Archie picked over the scraps. The meat did, in fact, taste like chicken.

Outside, distantly, something screamed in pain, then fell silent. The twittering of insects soon filled the void that followed. Even several minutes afterward, Anna could still feel her heart thudding uncomfortably fast against her chest, and she found the dinosaur meat was now churning uncomfortably in her stomach.

She could stand the silence no longer. She stared into the fire, fighting back fresh tears that threatened to erupt from her eyes. "I'm sorry. About your friend. He seemed...I'm sorry."

Syd nodded, but took several moments to respond. "I first met Tacoma while photographing his village for a Census report for the U.S. Government." He prodded more coals. "He was one of the few elders in the village who spoke English. Despite all the horrors he had seen, he still had hope that his people might one day return to their way of life."

She was surprised. This was the first she was hearing Syd voluntarily talk of his life. He never spoke about his past. He barely spoke at all. "You're a photographer?"

Syd pursed his lips, seemed to consider if he'd made a mistake, then offered up the information. "Merely an amateur. My daddy was, though. Back in the day."

"You chose not to follow in his footsteps?"

Syd shrugged. "When I was five years old, there was a gunfight outside my daddy's studio in Tombstone between the Earp boys and the Cowboys."

"I've heard of that," Anna said.

She remembered reading a pulp novel about the Gunfight at the O.K. Corral when she was still a very ill teenager. They had been wildly popular in London Society at the time, and though her friends had preferred such lurid gothic dramas as *Varney the Vampire* and *Werner the Were-Wolf*, Anna, who had lived so much of her life in the shadow of death, much preferred the cowboy stories about life on the wild frontier. The gunfights. The romance.

Grateful for the literary distraction, she started rambling off some details of the story as she had read about it, but Syd interrupted her.

"That's not exactly how it happened." It took Syd a moment to gather his thoughts before speaking again. "Our studio fronted Allen Street and had a rear entrance lined with stalls on Fremont. That's where the shootout actually took place—in the narrow lot on the side, a few doors down from the corral. But anyway…"

Syd threw some ashes on the fire before continuing. "My daddy was wounded in the crossfire. Didn't kill him. It was the sepsis that did him in a week later. I stayed with him, watched over him—me and my ma. But the doctors couldn't do shit. Excuse me." He paused as he remembered. "After that…well, the studio was finished."

Anna put a hand on her throat. "What did you and your mother do?"

"Ma married a widower and we moved to his farm. Not long after, I had me three brothers."

Anna smiled. "So things worked out." When he didn't immediately answer, she persisted. "They did work out?"

Syd kept his face carefully neutral as he stared into the fire. "The man she married was a pretty mean drunk. Used to beat me and my brothers. Beat my ma to within an inch of her life a coupla times 'fore I stopped him."

Anna stared blankly down at her hands resting in her lap. Syd didn't add anything to his story, but Anna could only imagine. She felt her heart clench inside for him. No wonder he became a lawman. In a place as huge and lawless as the Arizona Territory, it was difficult to find and keep good lawmen—men willing to do what was right and hard. According to the pulp novels she had read, good lawmen were made, not born. Men like Sydney Fly. So he had his reasons for enforcing the law. She only wondered if he was truly happy as a lawman.

She cast about for something to say, and finally squeaked out, "Do you ever think about it? The photography?"

Reaching into his rucksack, which he still had by some miracle, Syd pulled out a small, portable Bijou field view camera with lantern slides. Anna had heard of them and seen them advertised in catalogs, but had never seen one up close.

Syd let her examine it. "Not sure we'll be able to stand still long enough for me to get any decent pictures, but if we do…" He shrugged, leaving it at that.

"You want to go back into pictures."

Syd didn't respond, but he pressed his lips firmly together, which Anna took as an affirmative. Anna lifted the camera, which was lighter than she had anticipated, and aimed it at the opposite wall of the cave. The lenses inside magnified everything and made the image on the wall there jump out at her. With an exclamation, she set Syd's camera down, bounced up, and hurried to the opposite wall.

Syd turned his head to follow Anna as she went to examine the barely-legible symbols scratched into stone by what was likely a sharp rock. "What are those?"

"The Greek alphabet," Anna said. "Edmond wasn't just a big-game hunter. He was a scholar, as well. He taught them to me while I was ill." She stopped and turned to him. All her fatigue had suddenly vanished in one fell swoop. "Do you know what this means, Syd? Edmond carved these! He knew I would come. He knew I would know what they meant!"

Syd squinted at the chicken scratch. "You sure…?"

"Yes!" Anna had to keep herself from jumping up and down. "They're directions. He's saying he went northeast from here…" She followed up by pointing out different parts of the symbols.

Without saying anything more, Anna raced to the fire and started kicking dirt and rocks over it. Archie, roused by all the excitement, fluttered over her head as she worked.

"Wait just one second there..." Syd growled, standing up to grab her arm and halt her. "What the hell do you think you're doing, woman?"

Anna jerked her arm loose. "Getting out of here. We have to go northeast, Sheriff! If we go now, maybe we can catch up with him!"

"We're not going out there in the dark! Are you daft?" Syd yelled, his voice bouncing off the walls of the cave.

Anna stopped and set her hand on her hips. "How dare you? I—"

A high-pitched screeching noise interrupted their argument and made them both turn toward the blackness at the back of the cave. Anna spotted some queer side-to-side movement before slowly realizing what it was.

Rearing up at least seven feet was a gigantic centipede that she immediately recognized as the once thought to be long-extinct prehistoric arthropod *Arthropleura*. It clicked and buzzed, and its antennae flickered with interest as it unwound itself from a tight, defensive ball and started toward them, undulating over the rocks. Undoubtedly, it had been disturbed by their yelling. Its little legs ticked over the rocky ground as it slithered in their direction.

Anna couldn't help herself. Despite the unladylike nature of it, she started to scream with fresh new horror.

Syd muttered one of his most graphic expletives, grabbed her wrist in one hand, his rucksack in the other, and together, before the monster could reach them, the two of them fled like hell from the cave and into the midnight jungle, and to hell with the consequences.

16

Too Close for Comfort

A few hours later, Anna jerked away, almost tumbling out of the tree that she and Syd had taken refuge in shortly after they'd become hopelessly lost in the jungle night. The tree, a kind of primeval proto-pine, was huge and sprawling with strong branches, and they had managed to scramble up the roughened, scaly bark to the first thick limb and settled in the crotch. Gigantic insects buzzed past their faces, while large, heavy, mystery animals swayed by far below, oblivious to the tasty humans directly above them. It wasn't long before they started clinging to one another despite the inappropriate nature of it all.

There was no bloody way she was going to get any sleep tonight. "I don't like large insects," Anna said in a scorched whisper.

Syd surprised her. "Neither do I. Particularly whatever the hell that was back there. What the hell *was* that?"

"Giant centipede," she managed to stutter out. "Most paleontologists believe it was entirely herbivorous. That…that it only ate plants."

"Do you believe that?"

She was trembling so hard that the tree was shaking around them. "Excuse my American, but hell no."

Down below, something big was rustling through the under-brush. Anna couldn't see what it was, but it was large, and there seemed to be more than one. The hump of a spine rose up, followed briefly by an ugly, oversized head full of razor-sharp teeth and two horns projecting from above the eyes. It looked like the devil, if the devil was a dinosaur.

She gasped a quick breath at the sight.

"What...?" began Syd, but she quickly reached around and planted a grimy hand over his mouth.

"Shhh..." she hissed. "It's them. It's Mister and Missus..."

"The...what did you call them?"

"Carnotauruses."

The pair of carnivores must have heard their voices because they stopped, making grunting noises to each other. The brush shook violently, and Anna almost squeaked in alarm when she saw a long, reptilian tail lift up briefly from the brush and Mister and Missus glanced side to side before moving on, unable to pinpoint the exact location of their voices.

Letting out a sigh, Anna dropped her hand from Syd's mouth. They were very close together, their arms wrapped around each other. She could feel his breath on her cheek, his heart flitting against her side through the wall of his ribs. Anyone from London who'd seen them like this would have been outraged at the sight. They would have said she'd ruined herself, that she was a doxy. No man worth his mettle would marry her if he knew how she'd been conducting herself of late.

And that made her happy. That made her giddy with pure freedom. No expectations. No rules. Despite all the horrors she'd experienced, particularly in the last twenty-four hours, she realized that she felt really alive for the first time in her life. Really, her reaction was ridiculous and inappropriate, and she hoped to God that Syd didn't notice.

She cleared her throat and he grumbled something as he shifted on the branch, putting a few inches between them. He was either very sunburned or he was blushing. Either way, it was rather becoming on him. "Let's get out of here before Mister and Missus come back."

"Yes," she agreed. "Let's."

17

Blood to Blood

The jungle closed in all around them as they moved sluggishly through the thick, thorny brush, weaved around the thick trunks of the coniferous trees, and tried to avoid the huge, ground-hugging pitcher plants with their purple, orchid-like flowers and slightly sentient vines.

It was difficult. The heat was hellish and unrelenting. Syd had to bushwhack his way through with the Bowie knife on his hip while trying to remain as quiet as possible, plus the vines of the human-sized pitcher plants kept slithering over Anna's feet with insinuating interest, making her jump at the contact. The vines did not seem capable of actually grappling her, but their snake-like movements were nonetheless disconcerting.

And then there was the fauna. Dinosaurs. Anna had to force herself to think the word, it was so fantastic. Occasionally, small raptors dove through the underbrush—quick little bird-like dinosaurs covered in proto-feathers and big crests who twittered busily as they darted this way and that, snapping at large insects and gobbling frogs and other small prey. They would appear suddenly, out of seemingly nowhere, and, at times, it wasn't usual for Anna and

Syd to find themselves completely surrounded. Then, seconds later, they were gone without disturbing even a leaf on a tree. Thankfully, they were as small as chickens and too shy to attack anything larger than a dragonfly.

Anna kept expecting Archie to take off after a flying insect and never return, having found his kin in the jungle, but even though he disappeared periodically, they always found him just ahead, sitting in a tree, waiting for them and chattering with excitement. He never wandered very far.

The heat was the worst part of Blood Valley. Tight and oppressive like a hot, furry blanket around them both. Syd's shirt was entirely soaked through and clung to his rather impressive physique, while Anna's knickers and skirts stuck to her like an annoying second skin. Days ago, she had loosened her corset, but during the last break to relieve themselves, she had wriggled out of it and tossed the whalebone monstrosity aside. Still, she was drenched in sweat as they moved steadily northeast, much too slow for her liking, and, often enough, she had to stop just to get her breath properly.

They stopped to allow Syd to struggle with a particularly thorny bush in their path. "Maybe I ought to take over for a while."

Syd, looking exhausted, turned to her with the Bowie. "This isn't ladies' work."

"I can do it," she insisted. "I'm stronger than I look."

Syd shrugged.

It was harder than she thought. After only fifteen minutes of slashing through the thick, fecund underbrush with the pitifully small knife, Anna started feeling dizzy from the heat and lack of water. She stopped to drink from her canteen, only to discover the water was burning hot from the sun. She choked.

Syd took the knife from her. "I think I see water up ahead. Let me take over."

"No!" Anna bellowed, grabbing his arm. "I can manage it. I told you."

He let out his breath in exasperation. "You're much too thin, and you're ready to drop."

"I'm not too thin!" Her voice was reedy and desperate. Those were words she had heard all of her life. "I'm strong and I can do it!"

She grabbed the Bowie, but her sunburned fingers could barely close around the handle. Her palms were calloused and stung with sweat, and the skin of her knuckles was raw and bleeding.

He gave her a droll look. "You can ask for help, if you need it. It's allowed, you know."

"I'll bloody do it!" she said through gritted teeth. "I brought us here. I'll get us fresh water."

She began hacking wildly at the underbrush while Syd leaned back a safe distance from her. Her limbs had almost no strength, but she still had her resolve—and a need to see Edmond at any cost. She hacked and slashed until the vegetation began falling away and her arms felt like they were made of lead. By then, she was ready to drop, and when they finally stepped out into a clearing near a large lake, she was too dizzy to stand upright. She started pitching forward.

Syd caught her and bundled her up in his arms.

"I can do it..." she insisted, wheezing asthmatically. She struggled feebly as he easily carried her the rest of the way to the edge of the water. "I can walk if I have to."

"I know you can, Anna," he said, setting her down on the rocky shore and crouching low to wet his handkerchief.

He dabbed her burning brow with ice-cold water. Anna sighed in response. The sudden coolness after the long, hot trek made her feel better, almost giddy. After they drank their fill and had cooled down some, Anna said something very un-Anna-like.

"Do you want to swim?" She started reaching for her buttons.

"I don't think that would be such a good idea," Syd answered with his customary dryness.

"Oh." She was about to apologize profusely for her forwardness when Syd smirked ever so slight at her embarrassment and pointed out across the lake.

At the opposite end of it were a collection of tall, ragged rocks —volcanic refuse. An enormous creature was emerging from the water and creeping sideways up the sharp incline. It was as large as an Indian elephant and covered in a gigantic, bright red shell that shimmered wetly under the sun. She recognized it immediately as a monstrous crab.

"Ooohhh..." she said again, and quickly scrambled away from the lake as she watched the crab crawling over a ridge, followed by another, which had something peculiar in one of its claws. It looked like a large femur bone with a chunk of meat still clinging to it. A dinosaur bone? Anna couldn't be certain.

Syd stood up and his hand brushed his gun butt. "Imagine if we could get one of those beauties. We'd eat like kings."

He made a good point, and, in response to his words, Anna's stomach growled so loudly she was actually embarrassed. Standing up, as well, she started looking around for a possible weapon, a spear or maybe some large stones that she could throw at the crabs. Then the first crab turned to rebuff the second one following after it, clacking its free claw at its face, and she spotted the human skull in its other claw. She swallowed against the bile in her throat.

Syd froze and stared at the crabs tussling over the human re-mains, his hand stuck on the gun butt. For the first time, he looked truly nauseated.

Seconds later, an enormous creature burst from the lake in a thresh of white water. It was as large as a small ship and distinctively crocodilian, with a long, teeth-lined snout—though far, far larger than any crocodile that Anna had ever seen. Its eyes flashed red and its scutes glittered wetly under the noonday sun as it clashed its enormous jaws together, catching one of the crabs by the shell and dragging it under so quickly that, seconds later, the pond was still once more as if no act of violence had ever been perpetuated there.

A few seconds passed while Anna and Syd worked on composing themselves and getting their galloping hearts back under control. Syd indicated a small, circling pteranodon. "Want to try one of those instead? We'll find another cave and cook it up. Just not any with bugs in it."

Still clutching her chest, Anna said, "Yes. Yes, all right."

| 18 |

Land of Terror

Anna and Syd moved steadily up a steep ridge to clear the brush and then took shelter under an overhanging rock formation. Syd laid down flat on his back, trying to get a bead on one of the smaller birds. Anna stood nearby, acting as a lookout in case any of the bigger predators put in an appearance. Both of them hoped that Syd's long colt had enough stopping power to kill the bird. If they just wounded it, things were apt to not end very well for any of them.

"It's clear," Anna said, surveying their immediate environment.

"Fingers crossed."

"Everything crossed," Anna answered. Her stomach rumbled again.

Syd made the shot. The bird screeched before dropping like a lead weight out of the sky and landing in some brush. Syd rolled nimbly to his feet. "Let's go get 'er before some predator comes alone."

Together, they started back down the ridge, moving slowly to keep from skating over loose rocks and losing their footing. Anna hiked her skirts up. She could almost taste the pteranodon already.

The bird had landed near a stream. It lay crumpled like an insect, its wings twisted and beak half-open. Syd had managed to hit it in the throat, a quick kill, and its blood trickled into the moist, fecund earth.

Before they even approached it, Syd had his Bowie knife out. "Obviously, we won't be able to take the whole bird, but we can take what meat we can carry."

Anna nodded and started ripping the hem of her skirts to use as an extra rucksack for their trophy. She wasn't even done before a cry split the air—loud, grating...and very hungry-sounding. She stiffened, stopped what she was doing, and pointed toward a stand of trees. "Syd...look!"

A large predatory bird had stepped out of the tree line. It stood very still, observing them. Anna felt a chill. It was nothing like the little raptors they had encountered in the forest earlier that day. This specimen was ten feet tall, at least, and possessed of a powerful, S-shaped neck, keen-looking eyes, a huge, sharply hooked beak, and equally formidable-looking talons. Its entire body was covered in brown proto-feathers, and it sported a huge red crest.

Archie, perched on Anna's shoulder, squealed in alarm and hid his face in her hair. The creature remained where it was, moving not a muscle. It looked at them with such avarice that it took Anna a moment to place it in her books on prehistoric bestiary. "T-Terror..." she said.

Syd lifted his gun out of his holster very carefully and slowly. "What?"

"Terror..." Anna repeated. She swallowed. Hard. Her throat clicked. She couldn't seem to look away from the bird, which was standing on one leg and was so still, even its feather coating wasn't moving. It didn't look real. More like a painted statue. "Terror...Bird. They were apex predators. Carnivores. Other animals lived in terror of them, hence the name. Terror Bird."

"Well, shit." Syd pulled his gun loose a little further.

"They have very, very good eyesight, and, according to my books, hunt by movement."

Syd stopped and held very still. "Does it see us?"

"I'm not sure." Anna could feel the sweat running down her face, could hear her own heart flitting against her ribs. She tried to hold very still, but the more she thought about it, the harder it seemed to do. She tried to adjust her balance, but gravel crunched under her boot heel.

The Terror Bird twitched at the sound and angled its gigantic, frightening head her way. It clacked its jaws and twittered.

"Does it see me?" Anna whispered. "Does it…?"

It made that ear-splitting cry again, which was quickly answered by another, similar, cry from deep within the darkness of the jungle. Seconds later, another Terror Bird suddenly appeared, then another. Heads suddenly popped up all over, all heavily armed with hooked beaks and tall, red crests.

"Yeah," Syd whispered miserably. "I think it sees you. Run!"

In the Mouth of Madness

Anna and Syd thrashed through the underbrush. Syd kept a solid hold on her wrist, guiding her as they dove headlong through the giant ferns and brambly bushes. He was much taller than she, his strides longer. It took everything Anna had to keep up with him. But ahead, as a gigantic coniferous tree suddenly rose up before them, Syd was forced to let her go. Seconds later, he was gone, and Anna was alone, running as fast as her exhaustion would allow.

It wasn't enough. She could hear the Terror Birds behind her, squalling and twittering as they cut through the jungle with far more grace than she ever could. Still, Anna panted and pumped her legs, Archie shrilling as he glided along behind her as if encouraging her to run faster, faster. The shrubbery was as tall as she was, and the jungle whipped her face as she ran with blind panic toward what looked like another cave entrance up ahead, about a quarter of a mile away and up a steep, rocky ridge. Could she make it that far? And if she did, would the birds follow? Could they climb the ridge? She didn't know, but it was all she had.

Her ragged hem got in the way, and, within seconds, she found herself pitching forward. She landed hard on her face and lay there, heart kicking her in the ribs like a mule, but unable to move. She was terrified if she stood up, the Terror Birds would be on her in seconds.

Archie screamed, leading the birds on.

Anna held her breath as a half dozen giant birds soared over her and disappeared into the brush ahead, barely disturbing the vegetation. She continued to lay there for some minutes, panting into the wet earth until she heard a series of gunshots that she just knew was Syd. Slowly pushing herself up, she shoved the long tangles of her muddy hair out of her eyes and glanced around.

She seemed to be alone.

Syd. Was he all right? She had no way of knowing.

Dear God, what if the Terror Birds had trapped him? What if that gunshot was Syd going down for the last time? Scrambling, she got to her feet, weaving in the heat and all the horror she was experiencing. She was blind with sweat and terror and she wasn't even sure what direction to take.

"Have to keep going," she told herself and took off ahead, in the direction of the Birds...and ran straight into Syd, bouncing off his wide, thickly muscled chest.

"Syd!"

He caught her by the wrists as she began to crumble, pulling her back to her feet. His grip was almost painfully strong, but she didn't mind in the least. He was alive! She almost cried with relief, but Syd put a finger to his lips.

"I shot one," he panted, his face shiny-red with sweat as he glanced around them. "And...they look to be...eating it. I think they're cannibals. Let's go."

They started racing toward the ridge with the cave entrance. Anna could hear the Terror Birds rummaging around in the thick underbrush not far from where they were, squalling, clawing, and fighting over the bloody remains of their brethren. The sound only drove her on to cover the final hundred yards to the cave.

They tumbled inside and Syd dropped his rucksack. Anna slid to her knees with exhaustion while Syd went about the business of checking out the back of the cave for oversized centipedes and other unwanted beasties. The last thing they needed was to be taken unawares by another huge arachnid.

"Anything?" Anna asked, panting and coughing. She stayed on hands and knees, listening to the distant drip-drip of water on stone and worked on catching her breath. "Syd?"

No answer.

Anna sat up. "Syd? Syd!" she screamed.

Dear God, what now? She started scrambling to her feet when Syd suddenly appeared out of the dark, smirking as he held up a small green lizard he'd caught.

Finally, she thought. Something too small to want to eat them.

"It's clear," he said. He gave her a smirk as the little animal writhed around his wrist. "And it looks like there's a cave system back there. How about after dinner we check it out?"

"You want to go deeper into the cave?"

"It's either that or back out there." Syd nodded toward the jungle. "And I don't think I can outrun those big birds. Can you?"

***

After dinner, they walked slowly and in single file along the cavern, Anna's hand on Syd's arm. The cave was almost pitch-black, but the lichen clinging to the walls gave off its own ghostly phosphorescent glow. It wasn't much. Enough to see maybe five feet ahead, no more. As they moved from the main system and into a series of smaller tunnels, Syd kept his colt close at hand and continuously marked the walls with his Bowie knife.

Anna was impressed with Syd's ingenuity. The idea of becoming turned around and lost in these narrow tunnels was terrifying. Who knew how long the cave system was? It was possible it covered all of Blood Valley, and maybe even beyond it.

"As a child, I never used to be afraid of the dark," Anna said, talking for the sheer comfort of hearing something other than the desolate dripping of water that was slowly, over millions of years, eroding the stone around them—and driving her mad. "Edmond was afraid. Not me. I never understood why. Edmond was so brave otherwise."

She laughed a little at the memories of Edmond hiding under his covers as a child during a thunderstorm. "Edmond was fine with facing down a savage lion on the Serengeti, but he couldn't stand the dark."

"And you?" Syd asked. She was surprised by his interest. "Are you afraid now?"

She thought about that. "I don't know…no. I'm not afraid. Actually, I'm finding all of this a little bit exciting."

It was true. She wasn't underestimating the dangers of Blood Valley or making light of their losses, but something about it—the primitive, heart-pounding wildness of it—really did speak to her. She felt like this place had been waiting for her since forever, like she had always been meant to come here.

And there was something else. She didn't feel sick. She wasn't coughing and hacking like the sick little girl she had once been. In fact, she felt better physically than she had for a long, long time. When she finally saw Edmond—and she knew she would—she was going to tell him all about her adventure, about saving Syd from the pterosaur, and him saving her from the Terror Birds, and then she was going to ask—no, demand—that he take her with him on his next big safari.

She wanted to see Africa and India and all the unsafe places. The beautiful, wild, dangerous places. And then, when she was done, she would come back to the colonies. Maybe she would marry a cowboy and live like a frontierswoman.

She wondered if Syd was willing to show her what it took to survive in America. "Syd…" she began, but he suddenly went so still she almost plowed into him. "What is it?"

"Look down."

She did. It took her eyes a moment to pick out the dark, shiny drops of blood on the rocky ground. She swallowed, said, "Whose…whose do you think it is? Do you think it's some animal? Something…wounded?" She knew a wounded animal could be unpredictable.

Syd cocked his colt. "I mean to find out before we go any farther. Stay here."

"No."

He turned to face her, eyebrows raised.

She pulled her gun/sword from the sash around her waist. "I'm going with you."

"Anna…"

"I'm going, Syd! So let's get on with it, shall we?"

Something about her voice or poise must have convinced him that she wasn't about to be ordered into a corner like some fainting female, because he sighed and closed his eyes briefly. "Fine. Just don't shoot me with that contraption of yours."

Anna smiled. "I promise I won't shoot you."

"And be quiet from this point on."

She frowned but didn't respond.

They moved ahead, moving slowly, following the trail of blood drops.

The narrow tunnel slowly expanded as they moved along. Soon enough, they found themselves standing in a cavern as large as an amphitheater full of high, rocky shelves, stalactites, and a myriad of smaller tunnels leading away to other places. In the center of the cavern was a huge, still lake of dark water.

Anna eyed it suspiciously. She wondered if what was bleeding had come from that lake…or, perhaps, had *gone back into it.* Between the glowing lichen and the reflective nature of the water, the whole cavern was cast in perpetual light that made the space glow like a bright full moon. She could see everything clearly, every shadow, every mysterious scuttling thing, not that that made her feel any better about her surroundings. She clutched the gun/sword in both hands as a rather large spider the size of a terrier crawled over a boulder beside her.

She hated spiders. She had to press a hand over her mouth to keep from making any nervous sounds. A low, throaty moan escaped her anyway. Syd turned to her, frowning, and Anna blushed and threw her shoulders back, unwilling to be defeated by something as silly as a spider—large though it might be.

Syd flattened himself to the wall of the cavern, and Anna followed his lead. They crept along beneath a shelf of rock that hung down about seven feet above them. They tried to stay to the shadows and not appear too obvious a target for any hungry predators that might be living in the cavern. Anna shuffled over the rocky ground, trying to walk silent, though every little sound echoed like they were in a cathedral. Even their collective breathing seemed huge in this place.

A pebble dropped down to the ground from above. Anna and Syd both stopped dead in their tracks and waited, hearts knocking. A busy shuffling sound from above them on the rocky shelf made their spines stiffen in response. Another pebble dropped and pinged off into the darkness.

Syd pointed up. Anna nodded. Syd got his gun ready. So did Anna.

More scuffling noises. Whatever was up there sounded big and was pretty obviously on the move.

Anna felt her blood run cold, and she closed her eyes and sent up a quick prayer. *Please don't let it be one of those horrid Terror Birds.*

Her fingers hurt where she was gripping her weapon. Still, she watched Syd for an indication of what they were going to do. She wanted to help, but she had sense enough to know she had little experience in these matters.

Syd nodded, pointed up, and with his free hand counted off on his fingers. *One...two...three!*

The two of them jumped out from under the shelf, turned, and aimed their weapons up.

"Wait!" a man shouted in a panic, throwing up his hand. He was standing balanced on the ledge and weaving precariously as he sought to keep his balance. His face was pasty white and powdered with dust, and his clothes—once quite posh—were filthy as if he'd been crawling through the cavern for hours.

"Don't shoot!" he begged. "Bloody hell, what are *you* two doing here?"

Adam Bell. She recognized the scoundrel immediately. And if there was one thing she hated more than spiders, it was scoundrels.

| 20 |

Finding Edmond

"**Y**ou!" Anna shouted as the man who claimed to be the descendant of Robin of Locksley jumped down off the ledge in his long, dusty gambler's coat. The very sight of him boiled her blood.

"You...you cur!" Anna flew at him, knocking him over easily. "You burned our camp!" she cried, punching him square in the cheek where he lay there in the dust. He coughed in response and put his hands up to defend himself, but he didn't strike her in return.

"You took our horses. You almost killed us!" She punched him again, in the opposite cheek, shrieking like a madwoman.

That's when Syd lunged and pulled her off of him. She writhed and kicked, trying to get him to drop her, but he was stronger than she, unfortunately. "Let me go, Syd. Let me go immediately! I'm going to end him!" She started biting his hand, then realized how ridiculous she must seem.

Instead, she went limp in his arms and together they dropped to the ground, where Anna sat, eyeing the bastard in front of her as he worked to find his feet. There were two red spots appearing on his stupidly handsome face. Anna took satisfaction from that.

"Syd, I'm not a child. You can let me go," Anna finally sighed.

Adam Bell grinned at her in a smug way, even gave her a little finger wave.

"I know," Syd said, gently letting her go.

Anna, exhausted after everything they had endured, and starved half out of her mind, just slumped to the ground.

It was Syd who stood up, took a deep breath, and lunged at Adam. He grabbed the smaller man by the throat, slamming him against the nearest stone wall. Adam, almost a head shorter than Syd and slight of build, grimaced in pain, but Syd wasn't giving an inch.

"You two-bit horse thief! You belong on a gallows!" Turning, he threw Adam easily, and the man tumbled head over heels, landing on the muddy banks of the underground lake.

Grunting, Adam slowly pushed himself up. His derby was crooked on his head, and he was sitting in a pool of mud. He tried to find his feet but slipped in the mud and dropped down again. Holding up a hand, he said, "Look, mate, I'm sorry about the camp..."

"Sorry, my ass," Syd seethed. His eyes were narrow, his fists shaking, his breath hissing in and out of his mouth. Anna had never seen him so angry, and it was terrifying to witness because Syd seldom even raised his voice. He wasn't like Anna; his anger was all burning cold steel like a drawn weapon. He was a truly dangerous man, she realized. One that someone crossed only at their own peril.

Before she could say something, or even gasp in response, Syd was on Adam, dealing him a series of left hooks that drove him back farther and farther into the lake, the water splashing all around them. They rolled around, one on top of the other, but it was obvious that Adam didn't have a prayer in fighting back. Syd punched and kicked him like a toy. Adam yelled as he was driven into the water, only to be hauled up by Syd's big first and effortlessly pummeled into the water once more.

Adam was a swindler, a roué, and most certainly on Worthington's payroll. Anna couldn't stand the sight of the man, but after a few minutes of Syd tossing Adam around like a straw man, she started feeling a little bit sorry for him. Who knew what his story was? He might have come from a rough background. He probably lived for his own selfish purposes. Was he a bad person of the same caliber as Worthington? She didn't know, but she decided she couldn't judge.

She took a few steps toward the water. "Syd!" she said, raising both hands. "Syd, stop!"

Surprisingly, he did as she asked.

Anna looked down on the sorry visage of Adam Bell. "Enough. I think there's been more than enough bloodshed today..." She started to say more when she noticed something lying on the ground, having fallen out of Adam's pocket during all the fisticuffs. She looked at it, thinking she was imagining things. Then, after a long moment, she approached it hesitantly.

Kneeling, she picked up the pocket watch, clutching it with care like something that might bite her. Turning it over, she saw the initials carved on the back: *E. T. M. R.*

Edmond Theodore Melville Rutherford.

"Where...?" She held the watch up by the chain as her heart and stomach began to sink. "Where did you get this?"

Adam, sitting soaking wet on the ground, tested his jaw, which was bruised. He gave her a disgruntled look, all his smug good humor gone. He was a rumpled mess and his lip was split. He spit blood, and, for once, just looked tired and defeated.

"Why?" was all he said. Again, he touched his jaw, and winced. "What do you bloody care where I got it?"

"Because it's my brother's pocket watch!" Anna said, a feeling of dread gathering like a burning stone in her belly. "And I need to know where you found it! Show me!"

* * *

Adam stumbled along, walking around the edge of the lake with Syd at his back, prodding him with his colt whenever he slowed his pace. Adam grumbled out a curse but kept walking until they reached the opposite shore. There, he pointed down a narrow corridor of stone. "I found him there when I first found this place." He sounded almost inarticulate with his swollen jaw.

Anna, who had been following the two men, stepped away from Syd and gripped the pocket watch tight. "Who?" Her heart was thudding so loudly she was afraid they could hear it.

"The bloke," said Adam to Anna. "Not tall, but blonde. He looked like you."

"You found...?" she began, but found she couldn't finish the sentence. Instead, she turned to look at the tunnel.

Syd immediately moved forward to put a hand on her shoulder. "Anna..."

She brushed it away. Her eyes were dry, but there was something like a walnut stuck in her throat. "No...I need to see. I need to go alone." She looked up at him, and after a hesitant moment, Syd nodded.

The tunnel was darker than the cavern, but there was just enough lichen to see adequately by. Anna started down the tunnel, the gun/sword in one hand, the pocket watch in the other. She put one foot in front of the other, forcing herself on even though she didn't want to go. Didn't want to know. If she didn't know, she could go on. She could have hope.

I can't be a child, she told herself over and over. *I have to know. I have to see.*

Slowly, step by step, the narrow tunnel opened up into a kind of stone pocket, a dead end with nowhere to go. The space was about the size of her bedchamber at home, and the walls smooth, eroded by millions of years of dripping water. The lichen grew wild here, clumping together to form powerful lighted patterns.

In the back, under an outcropping of light, she found Edmond.

Adam Bell, even being the outlaw he was, had done the right thing. He had covered Edmond with stones. He was an Englishman like she; he knew how to build a burial cairn when there wasn't enough loose earth to dig a proper grave. He had even designed a cross at the head of the grave with smaller stones.

She looked at the cairn for a long, long time. It didn't look real. It couldn't be real. She was almost tempted to run up to it, cast the stones away herself to see, but all she could do was stand there, clutching the pocket watch while Syd and Adam gathered around her.

Adam was terribly contrite for once. "The bloke...he was badly injured. I think...I think the big birds got to him, but he'd gotten away. I think he was hiding in here, but his injuries were just too much..." His voice faded away to nothing, and Anna listened to the rhythmic dripping of water on stone, endless and oblivious to all things living or dead.

This cave hasn't changed in millions of years, she thought as she slid to her knees at the foot of her twin brother's grave. Not much, anyway. A little erosion. Some fissure damage from earthquakes, but not much. It was strange how her mind turned to such mundane, scientific things in this moment.

"Edmond," she said after a moment. She clutched his pocket watch like a Rosary. "His name was Edmond. Edmond Rutherford. And he was my brother and the only real friend I've ever really had."

| 21 |

Beyond Escape

Anna sat shivering in front of the fire while Syd and Adam argued in the background. They were barking plans back and forth regarding about how they planned on getting out of the cave system without attracting the attention of the Terror Birds, but the little details went right over her head. All she could do was sit and shiver and wonder how she had come to be here, alone with these two madmen, while her brother lay under a cairn of rocks in another part of the cave.

How could she be so stupid as to be hopeful when she first came to this godforsaken place? Moreover, how had she not known that Edmond was gone? She was his twin. She should have *known*. She should have felt his passing. Instead, while she was blustering all over Dead Horse and acting like a silly schoolgirl around Sydney Fly, her brother—her Edmond—had been lying in this cavern, cold, alone, and fatally injured.

When she was seven and her illness was at its worst, she was convinced that God was calling her home. Edmond had stepped into her bedroom, carrying one of the kittens that had been born from the stable cat and said in a perfectly serious tone of voice that she would be all right.

"Don't be foolish, Anna. You won't die," he said. "We're twins. That means we have to die on the same day, and I'm not ready to die, so you can't, either."

Something about the deadly serious tone of his voice had made her laugh. He sounded like a prophet. They were supposed to die on the same day, yet here she was. Alive. She had failed him. She had failed Edmond. The realization stabbed her deep in the heart with a weapon no kinder than a knife.

The building pain made her grip her own shoulders and finally scream. She screamed loud and long, and when she was done, she dropped to her knees by the fire and simply rocked back and forth, sobbing like some weak-willed female in a novel of feverish romance.

The two men behind her stopped arguing and just hovered there while Anna sobbed and sobbed until she thought she might throw up.

Finally, Syd said, "Anna..." and started toward her. For once, he looked at a loss as to what to do, what to say. But before he could even make it halfway, Adam jumped in front of him.

"Just leave her alone, you cretin."

Syd stopped and glared at the smaller man. "What did you say?"

"You're a bloody cretin!" Adam shouted into Syd's face. "You don't know the first thing about what she's going through..."

Anna sat up straighter. She was surprised by Adam's venom. For a man who had recently been beaten to a near pulp by Syd, he didn't look half-scared of the man. The fact that she had done some of the beating on him only mystified her further. Why would he care what she was going through?

Syd grabbed Adam by the cravat. "You little punk...!"

"That's the answer for you, isn't it, mate? Don't like someone, smash their face in with your fists…"

"Stop it!" Anna screamed.

She could endure this no longer. She struggled to her feet and stumbled toward them, tripping over her ragged hem. "For the love of God, stop fighting! Do you know how much trouble we are in? *Do you?*" She glared first at one man, then the other.

Both of them suddenly looked cowed by her anger.

"There is no bloody way those birds are going to let us leave here alive!" she said, gesturing wildly around the cavern. "So, unless there's another way out of here, we're going to die down here with Edmond. Do you understand me? *We are going to die here in Blood Valley!*"

Her voice had reached a fever pitch. She stopped and took a few deep breaths, worked on calming herself. This was no way for a lady to act, she reminded herself. Edmond wouldn't have approved of her acting this way.

Adam sniffed against the congealing blood in his nose, then reached up and straightened his cravat. "We're not going to die. I'm going to get us out of here."

Both Anna and Syd turned to look at him.

"What did you say?" Syd said.

Adam ignored him and took a few steps toward Anna, extending his hand. "If you'll lend me Edmond's pocket watch, I think I can get us out of here."

Anna started to protest. It was obvious to her that he just wanted the watch, but Adam shook his head as if he were reading her thoughts. Spitting away a little blood, he went on at length about his plan. It wasn't a great plan as plans went. It wasn't even a good one, and it would most likely get him killed.

"I think you're mad," Anna said when he had finished. "Why would you do that? Why would you even helps us?"

It wasn't like they were friends. Hell, they weren't even allies.

"That bastard Worthington," Adam said, sniffing and wiping blood from his face. His voice had dropped a few octaves with his seething anger. He suddenly seemed a much more dangerous man. "He sent me and my men in as cannon fodder—just like Edmond. He knew the dangers, and still he sent us along, and without any proper weapons. And it got all my men dead. I know that now."

Anna didn't immediately catch on, but Syd nodded as he stood there, idly playing with the rig on his hip. "Worthington sent you and your men ahead so he could send the *real* caravan along behind ya'll. The first set of men were just a moveable feast to help the second caravan arrive safely."

"You and your men were expendable. You were always expendable," Anna said, finally catching on. "That means…"

"Worthington's men are probably on their way, or are already here," Adam said with a sharp nod. His eyes glittered in the firelight. Year of anger and betrayal flashed there, and Anna wondered if they hadn't misjudged Adam.

"He didn't mean for any of us to survive this, and when you two come face to face with the bloody son of a bitch, I want you to fill him full of holes for me."

| 22 |

The Nest

Anna and Syd followed Adam down the twist of tunnels that Adam said led to the surface. Adam told them earlier that he'd been down in these tunnels for hours—all night, at least, though he had no way of judging the time of day underground—and had had the time to explore them to some extent, which is how he found Edmond. In the process, he'd found one possible route of escape. The problem was, the Terror Bird's nesting grounds were directly above it. He'd planned on going the other way and taking his chances with any creatures lurking outside the cave entrance when Anna and Syd suddenly showed up.

"We could try the cave entrance now, I suppose," Anna suggested. "Maybe the birds are gone."

"Not going to work. Too many blind spots," Adam insisted. "They could ambush us from any angle in the jungle."

Anna grudgingly agreed that was a possibility—one that could get them very dead.

They walked single file with Syd holding aloft a makeshift torch that threatened to go out at any moment. At the outset, he'd wishing aloud he'd had been able to get a hold of some tree resin to keep the torch alight. At present, it was made of a thick stick, a bundle of Anna's hem, and some of Syd's gun oil as an accelerant. They'd had to do the best they could with very little to work with. Now, they had to guard the torch with their lives, if necessary. It might be their only defense against the birds.

A swift wind down the tunnel made their precious torch flicker and almost go out. Anna swore.

"You won't need fire," Adam reassured them. Despite being all banged up, he still cut a dashing figure in his long gambler's coat, and Anna though the spectacles he wore made him look adorable—despite the bruises on his face. She was starting to feel very badly about how she had treated him.

"There's no way we're getting out of here without a weapon," Syd insisted, sounding grumpy. He kept looking over at Anna, then at Adam, as if he suspected they were in cahoots with one another. It hadn't improved his mood any, that was for certain.

"Fine, gov, keep your caveman weapon, then. No skin off this nose," Adam said, laying two fingers to the side of his gracefully sloping nose.

Syd bristled at the way Adam was brushing him off, and Anna was suddenly afraid they would start fighting again in the middle of the cave tunnel, something she didn't think she could handle at the moment.

Thankfully, Adam moved on without saying anything more that might provoke Syd.

After about five minutes of walking, the tunnel grew brighter, and Adam pointed off in the distance. "Tickety-boo, we're almost there."

A few minutes later, they came to a stop under a large, moonlit hole cut into the rock ceiling by centuries of water erosion. Anna realized they had been down here all day and it was close to midnight, or even later. The hole, a kind of natural chimney cut into the earth, was about ten feet up and full of stars. It was not so far that someone tall like Syd couldn't reach it with a little stretching, and he started doing just that.

Handing Anna the torch, he approached the hole and reached an arm up toward the lip. He had to jump just a little to reach it.

"Wouldn't do that if I was you, mate," Adam said.

"Be quiet," Syd said, still sounding cross.

"Your funeral." With a shrug, Adam wandered away and sat down against the rock wall, his attention riveted on the ceiling.

Anna raised the torch so Syd could see the edge of the hole better as he jumped for it. Seconds later, Syd gave a shout and yanked his arm down.

Anna started. The sleeve of his coat was frayed and he was swearing under his breath at the blood running down his arm.

Seconds later, a loud crowing filled the chamber as one of the Terror Birds tried to stick its huge, parrot-like beak down the hole. Though just about wide enough for a slender man to slide through, it was too small for the gigantic bird to get more than half its head inside. It screamed in frustration while Syd and Anna jumped back.

Adam chuckled. "Told you, gov."

Syd swung around, blood dripping from the gash in his forearm and eyed Adam. He looked tired and impatient. "I ought to…"

Anna threw the torch down and got between the two men, putting her hands on Syd's chest to hold him back. She gritted her teeth. She didn't know what had gotten into him of late, but his behavior was completely unacceptable. "Settle down, Syd. We don't need another fight. Not now, of all times." She pushed him forcefully back.

Syd snarled and pointed at Adam. "He did that on purpose!"

"Not like you didn't deserve it, mate."

Dear Lord, she felt like a governess with two unruly children.

"Stop it!" she shouted, surprised by the force of her voice. "Stop acting like some spoilt child, Syd." Then she turned to Adam, who was grinning. "And you…stop baiting Syd!"

Adam stopped grinning and mumbled something unmentionable under his breath. It sounded like "Wanker."

Syd started forward, fists at the ready, but Anna blocked him, giving him a stern look.

"No!"

"Anna…"

"I said no," she repeated. "If you want to fight Adam like some bloody caveman, you have to go through me!" That settled him down. Sighing, she put her hands on her hips. "We have to figure out how many of those birds are up there."

"Ten," mumbled Adam from under his hat. He had set it on his face as if he were taking a nap. "There are ten."

"And how do you know that?"

Adam finally stood up, straightened his hat, and moseyed over to them, taking off his pince-nez. He handed them to Anna, who frowned with confusion. "Try them."

She did not expect anything special but gasped when she realized how they worked their magic. "I can see right through the ceiling!" She took them off and put them on again, thinking it was some trick of the light.

Finally, she looked them over very carefully. "Refractive lenses." She looked up at Adam. "Where did you get these?"

"I tinker."

"You made these?" She looked at him with brand new eyes. He didn't look like the sort who would "tinker," but then, she knew that appearances could be quite deceiving. Most people she met would hardly take her for a scholar and an archeologist. They usually treated her like some brainless butterfly.

She noticed Syd glowering at them both in one corner but chose to ignore him. "How? Are you an inventor?" She hadn't had many occasions to meet people like him with similar interests.

A corner of Adam's mouth quirked up in a half-smile. "Sometimes. When I have the time and shekels."

"How did you do it?"

"Well," he began, taking the glasses and showing her, "when you add a concave lens and then heat it to..."

"I'd hate to break up your little convention, but we should be doing something about those damned birds," Syd interrupted, sounding sour.

Anna put the glasses on. "Let me do it," she said, referring to the most dangerous part of Adam's plan.

Syd grabbed her by the sleeve. "Oh no, you don't."

Anna yanked her sleeve away. "I'm the smallest and fastest here. I can do it. I can run faster than Adam..."

"I don't care. I'm not letting you endanger yourself."

"That's not your decision to make, Syd."

"Anna..."

"How dare you? You're not my husband," she pointed out. "You don't get a say!"

"Someone has to tell you what's what—"

"Syd, I mean it," Anna stated empirically. "I can do this..."

She stopped speaking when she realized she couldn't find Adam anywhere. While they had been arguing, he'd been on the move. Glancing around, she spotted him pulling himself up through the hole using some kind of grappling hook on a wire he had up his sleeve. By looking through the special x-ray lenses, she could see an array of nests on the ground only a stone's throw from where Adam was hoisting himself through the hole. About half of them had birds sitting eggs. "Adam!"

"You guys better be ready to run," he said, yanking Edmond's pocket watch from the inside pocket of his coat where he had pocketed it without Anna noticing. It flashed in the moonlight, a perfect distraction.

"Adam! You're mad!" she shouted up at him, jumping up and down even though there was no way she was going to be able to reach him.

"You better believe it, chit."

Then the wiry young man was through the hole in the ceiling, and Anna flinched as she heard the hellish caterwauling of the Terror Birds.

| 23 |

Green Hell

"**G**ive us a bump up, Syd, yeah?" Anna commanded, and for once, Sydney Fly didn't give her a hard time. He just made a saddle with his hands so Anna could slip the toe of her boot into it. Syd bumped her up fast and hard. His strength was such that it brought her right to the edge of the hole.

She grappled with the edges, tearing her fingernails as she sought purchase, but managed to wriggle through. She bent this way and that like an inchworm to gain traction. As she writhed halfway out of the hole, she took in her surroundings.

Thankfully, no birds were in sight.

They were on a rocky volcanic slope that edged downward toward the river where they had encountered the monster crocodile, but high enough—and treacherous enough—that the larger animals like Mister and Missus and the herds of armored herbivores would have had difficulty traversing the landscape without slipping. It was the perfect place for the large birds to roost without attracting predation.

"Oh, God, Adam!" she said.

Currently, he was standing amidst the cluster of nests clinging to the rocky ridge, holding Edmond's pocket watch by the chain and catching the light of the full moon in its burnished clamshell and then flashing it at the nearest birds' faces.

The birds who had come to investigate what was done in the hole were squawking and weaving on their long legs and shaking their heads at the glare. The flashes of light were holding them at bay for the moment, but she knew it wouldn't last long.

Grunting, Anna extradited her bottom half from the hole and clambered to her knees on the rocky ridge, then turned and called down. "Syd! Give me your hand!"

"There's no way..."

"Just give it to me. Adam doesn't have much time!"

Syd, looking skeptical, raised his hand. Anna stuck both down the hole and took hold of Syd's. His hand dwarfed hers and she had her first misgivings. She pulled, but he was much too heavy to lift. Even using both hands and all of her strength, she couldn't find the purchase to lift him more than an inch off the ground before she lost her grip and his sweaty hand slid out of hers.

She fell back on the hard ground with an *oof* of air.

This was never going to work this way.

"Anna!" Syd called from below, his voice echoing. "Run! I'll find another way out!"

"I'm not going anywhere!" she responded stubbornly. She was dirty and sweaty, and her hands were bleeding. She was near tears with frustration, but she refused to leave Syd down in that godforsaken hole.

An idea came to her, and she clambered back to the hole and shouted down. "Your rucksack. Send it up!"

Syd looked confused but obediently tossed it up to her. Anna snatched at it and pulled it through, then tore it open. While he was showing her his camera last night, she had noticed a length of heavy-duty cordage in it, something no cowboy would leave home without. She liberated it and looked around for something to tie it to, but they were on a rocky slope and there were no trees or bushes nearby—no vegetation at all, for that matter.

Behind her, she heard Adam swear violently. "You two better bloody hurry up and stop ball dancing! These birds ain't too impressed anymore with the shiny thing."

Huffing and puffing, Anna finally chose to tie the rope around a large rocky outcropping, praying to God it would hold with Syd's full weight on it. Once she'd knotted it as best she could using a ship knot she remembered reading about in a book once, she tossed the rest of the rope down the hole. Without needing any encouragement, Syd took it and tied it around his waist, then nodded and started rappelling up the wall.

Anna knew it would take him some time to get up and out of the hole. She turned to lend Adam a hand.

Currently, he was surrounded on three sides by the giant birds. Long-legged and swift, they lunged back and forth, trying to get closer and closer to him. Each time they came within arm's length, Adam flashed the light from the watch into their eyes, making them squawk and flutter backward, but it was obvious by the bloodlust in their eyes that such juvenile tactics wouldn't hold them back for long.

Reaching to her hip, Anna liberated the gun/sword and stepped forward, checking her munitions. She only had a few shots left, not nearly enough to take out this lot, even if she hit every single target. Instead, she aimed the sword point at the birds and started barking at them to get back while stabbing precariously close to their faces.

"You crazy chit, what the hell are you doing?" Adam asked.

"Helping you?" She stabbed one of the ten-foot birds in the throat as it leaned into her. The bird shrieked and danced backward, raising its red crest and fluttering its tiny, undersized wings in agitation. Its mean, piggy eyes seemed to center solely on her, to see only her.

"I think you made it angry."

"Yes," Anna agreed. "It would seem that way."

The Terror Bird shrieked so loudly that Anna was afraid her eardrums would split and then lunged once more.

Anna screamed too in response. The sword point went into the bird's throat and a freshet of blood decorated the rocks at its feet. The bird gargled and weaved on its feet, not mortally wounded, but hurt enough to disorient it. Anna, sensing an opportunity, slashed at the bird's exposed neck. Shrieking, the bird reared back, the red wound in its throat gaping wide.

Syd was right about the Terror Birds. They were opportunists.

The other birds saw their wounded compatriot and went into a frenzy, jumping on the bird and driving it to the ground under their weight. Their hooked beaks snapped and ripped bloody chunks of flesh from the fallen bird.

"Cannibals," Adam said with surprise and some disgust. "They're bloody cannibals!"

"Which is good for us. Let's get Syd out of that hole."

Both turned back to their companion. Syd, meanwhile, was half in, half out of the hole in the ground. He had gotten stuck at the chest, the hole just a little too narrow for his burly body.

"Help me with him!" Anna shouted, dropping her weapon and taking Syd's hand.

Adam stood there and seemed to think about it for a moment as if unsure whether to help Syd or run off. She dearly hoped he didn't run off.

"Adam, hurry!" Anna shouted, and that motivated the man. With a shrug, he took Syd's other hand and pulled. Together, the two of them started wriggling Syd loose inch by painful inch.

Syd cursed as they dragged him from the hole in the ground. He collapsed onto his face as Anna and Adam let go of his arms. He was down only seconds before he grunted and pushed himself to his hands and knees, cursing under his breath. Anna and Adam turned to see what he was looking at.

The Terror Birds had almost entirely stripped their fallen comrade of meat and gristle. Bloody bones were all that were left. Now, they were looking for more.

Adam immediately whipped out the pocket watch and flashed it at them, but they seemed less than impressed by it this time, their hunger and bloodthirst too great. One darted right toward them, hooked beak wide open…only to scream as it was dive-bombed by what looked to be a small but fierce bird.

"Archie!" Anna cheered as the archaeopteryx whistled a scream and fluttered in the face of the predator threatening her. Despite his small size, his fierceness threw the bigger bird off his game and it lurched backward in surprise, snapping blindly at him. But it was unable to catch Archie.

"What the hell is that?" Adam barked.

"Anna's pet dinosaur," Syd said, using the rope he'd climbed out of the hole with like a lasso to bind and pull the feet out from under a Terror Bird creeping too close to them. The bird squalled as it went down on its side, flapping its little useless wings madly.

Meanwhile, the Terror Bird tracking Archie managed to clack its huge, hooked beak on one of Archie's long tail feathers. Archie squealed in terror as the feather was yanked out.

With a cry, Anna leveled her gun/sword at the predator and jerked the trigger, blasting a hole in the side of its head. The Terror Bird shrieked out of its beak and out of the side of its head as it dropped to the rocky ground, dead. The others descended on it immediately, ripping it to bloody ribbons, but she knew that wouldn't satisfy them for long.

"Let's go before they get any more ideas," she said as Archie alighted on her shoulder and hid behind her ear, wrapping his long, feathered but reptilian tail around her neck.

All three of them ran toward the green hell of the jungle.

World's End

They made the unanimous decision to keep moving no matter what. Their hope was that come morning, they would be far enough from the Terror Birds' nesting site to be of no interest to them anymore.

Syd was certain they had walked south, and if they kept doing so, they would eventually reach the outskirts of the Sonora once more. He seemed to know where he was going, so Anna and Adam followed his lead.

They walked wordlessly through the dense prehistoric undergrowth. Syd used Anna's sword to cut through the hardier vegetation since his Bowie had become dull from overuse. Around them, the jungle twittered with life, and unseen creatures slithered in and out of sight as they passed, but, thankfully, none was large enough to be a threat.

To Anna, the parched desert now seemed like paradise, and she couldn't wait to see the unforgiving deadpan once more. It was a killing land, to be sure, but it was still safer than Blood Valley. She couldn't wait to leave this land behind forever. She would have liked to have retrieved her brother's body before they left, but she knew that was quite impossible now. There was no way anyone could safely venture back into the Terror Bird's territory. It was a sheer miracle that any of them had survived at all.

She stumbled and fell against Syd, who turned to her, steadying her on her feet. "You're exhausted. We should take a break."

"I'm fine," Anna said peevishly. "I want to get out of here. Now."

"I think we should stop," Adam said, his first words since they had left the Terror Birds behind. He pulled up his sleeve to reveal a deep cut that looked infected and in need of stitches. It was red and swollen. It looked as if one of the birds had scratched him.

Anna ogled it. "You should have said something!"

"I want to get out of here, too." He sounded tired, and all his bluster was gone.

"Let's stop," Syd said, not giving anyone time to argue. There was a cave system up ahead, about a quarter mile out of their way. He pointed. "There."

They hiked toward it even as the sun started coming up, throwing sheets of light over the unfamiliar, primordial jungle. Anna refused to say as much, but she felt a great wave of relief when they finally reached the cave. She was hot and tired, and her feet hurt so badly she wasn't sure how she would walk the rest of the way out.

While Syd and Adam gathered sticks for a bonfire, Anna retreated to the back of the cave, keeping her weapon close at hand. "Clear," she called back once she'd done a full circuit of the cave and discovered it was a dead end, no mysterious tunnels and no strange creatures slithering around that were any larger than a mouse.

There was a pool of water only a little larger than a big puddle between a ring of jagged rocks where it had collected from some underground seep, and it was the most wonderful thing Anna had ever seen. She splashed cold water on her face and the back of her sunburned neck. She filled their canteens, then peeled off her safari boots and stuck her sore and bleeding feet into the soothing cold water.

She sat there at the water's edge, listening to the now-familiar drip-drip of water on rock, and just let herself cry into the elbow of her tattered shirt for a little while. She felt stupid and weak, but she couldn't help herself. Edmond was dead. The reality of it was only now sinking in. She would never see him again, not in this life. She would never hear his voice. He would never try to cheer her up again. And it was Worthington's fault. Worthington had sent him into this green hell...

A footfall behind her made her start and sit up straighter. She quickly wiped the tears away and pulled herself back together as Adam crouched down beside her to wash the wound in his arm.

"Let me take care of that for you," Anna said, trying to sound stronger than she felt at the moment.

"It's nothing," he insisted.

"It needs stitches. You could die from infection. Let me."

He flinched when she took his arm and rolled up the sleeve to reveal the wound, but she didn't think it was her handling that had caused his reaction. He acted afraid she would strike him again, and again she felt badly about the way she had treated him earlier.

What he had done to their camp in the Sonora hadn't been right, but her reaction hadn't been right, either. *Two wrongs don't make a right.* Something Edmond used to say when he was bullied by the other children or slighted by the high society he was supposedly a part of. She used to admire his enormous capacity for forgiveness.

Adam's wound was deeper than she had first noticed. It certainly needed care if he wasn't to die from sepsis before they ever got out of here. She said as much as she reached into her coat pocket and pulled out a small medic's case she had thought to bring with her.

"Are you a nurse?" Adam asked.

"No, but I've studied anatomy at university."

"You have a knowledgeable touch—like a nurse."

"I'm an archaeologist." She washed and debrided the wound as best she could, then used a vial of antiseptic on it before getting her suture set out, thankful for the busy work. At least it would keep her mind off her own troubles.

Adam was quite the trooper. He would have made the King's army proud. The muscles of his forearms jumped and contracted as she sewed his wound shut, but he never so much as grunted that he was in pain.

While she was bandaging him up, he said, "I've never met a female archaeologist before. I thought you were the daughter of an Earl?"

"I am." She didn't elaborate. "He doesn't approve."

"I can imagine." Adam flexed his arm. He stared down at it, looking very hangdog, suddenly. "I apologize for all of this, madam. I had no idea what breed of man Worthington is."

"Yes," she agreed, thinking about her brother. "Worthington is very good at blinding men with his money and his ambition."

"Money. The eternal evil," Adam groaned.

She waited, but when he didn't go on, she asked, "What do you need the money for?"

He looked surprise that she should ask. "Investment capital." He hesitated as if afraid he had said too much, then his expression softened as his thoughts went elsewhere. "We want to put a down payment on a ranch. Cattle, horse, maybe even some sheep, even though I hate the stupid bloody bastards."

"We," Anna said. "You have a girl?" She couldn't help but feel a little stab of disappointment at the news. Despite the bruises, Adam certainly wasn't hard on the eyes. Any woman would count herself lucky to catch a man as handsome as he.

He hesitated a long moment. Then, with a wistful smile, "Aye...a girl."

Anna smiled in response. Happy, Adam looked completely transformed. Young and boyish. Innocent. It almost didn't make her jealous to see. "I hope you get back to her very soon."

"Thank you, Lady Anna."

"So, you two getting married?" Syd asked gruffly from behind them. He was standing there with a couple of homemade spears in his hands and a disgruntled look on his face.

"Yes," Anna joked. "We're going to get a ranch and have many children. We may even get a little dog."

Syd didn't laugh at her jest. He kicked the ground. "Let's move out."

| 25 |

Battleground

"Y ou're being extremely rude," Anna said to Syd while they cut a fairly even swath through the jungle vegetation. Adam had disappeared a few minutes ago to relieve himself and she and Syd were alone for the moment, each armed with a weapon—Syd a spear, Anna her gun/sword.

Syd was watching a flock of pteranodons circling far above them. They hadn't acted forward just yet—Anna thought the trees were too thick for an aerial attack—but she wasn't putting it past them to find a way to make their lives a little more miserable.

"How am I being rude?" Syd finally responded.

"I don't like the way you've been speaking to me," Anna said, surprised by the hurt in her voice.

He tilted his head and squinted at her from under the brim of his hat. "Do you want me to address you as Lady Anna now?"

"That's not what I mean. I thought we were friends. Allies, at least."

"We are." He didn't specify which.

"Then don't speak to me so shortly. Or Adam."

"That punk."

"He's proven useful."

"He's still a punk. He'll come to no good end." He looked away briefly as something rustled in the undergrowth. He stiffened and his fingers tightened around the spear. Suddenly, a small raptor emerged, warbling and chasing a giant dragonfly.

He relaxed as it ran off. "You can do better than him."

It took her a moment to catch one, but when she did, Anna laughed.

"What's so funny?" Syd asked, sounding annoyed.

She thought about mentioning his jealousy, laying it all out for him, but then thought better of it. He was a man and wouldn't get it. She didn't want to embarrass him, and she was frankly too flattered to mention that Adam had someone waiting for him at home. "Nothing," she said, shaking her head. "Nothing..."

Adam came rushing back, breathless and wide-eyed, tucking his shirt into his trousers. He used his sleeve to rub the sweat off his brow. The jungle was like a sweltering green wall all around them. "I think I saw one of the birds. The big ones."

"Terror Birds?" said Anna, glancing around.

Syd stepped between them. "I thought we made it out of their territory?"

Adam looked annoyed. "Ten feet tall and a bloody red crest. I know what I saw!"

"We left those bastards miles behind us. They shouldn't be following us."

"Yeah, well, tell them that," Adam said.

"Maybe they're tracking us," Anna suggested and all eyes turned on her. She was supposed to have all the answers, after all. "We might have altered their territory by invading their nesting grounds the way we did."

"Well, shit." And Syd started bushwhacking like crazy.

They started out again, moving much faster this time, but it wasn't long until all three of them realized they weren't alone any longer. Anna felt the little hairs on the back of her neck stand up. Seconds later, the now-familiar screeching cry rang out, then the undergrowth began crunching as the birds cut through it much faster than they were.

Syd stopped and turned. "Keep going. I'm going to give those bastards some fresh meat to occupy them."

"They'll kill you, Syd!"

"They can try." With a determined look on his face, he hefted the spear in his hand, the head of which was made from a piece of sharp shale bound to the shaft with cordage.

There was no way Anna was leaving Syd to this place, not like how she'd had to leave Edmond behind. If he was going to fight, she was going to do so right beside him. Fight and live or fight and die, she was tired of running.

She swung around, ready to help Syd, when they all heard a deep bellow off in the distance. They had heard it only once before, but Anna would have known that sound anywhere. She put a hand on Syd's shoulder. "I have a better idea. Follow me."

The two men looked at her uncertainly, but when she started shouldering her way through the jungle, they soon followed, staying close behind her.

Adam stopped dead in his tracks when he saw what direction they were taking. "Why are we running *toward* the big bellowing, threatening sound?"

Syd, to Anna's relief, came to her defense. He jogged past Adam, wielding the spear, his rucksack on his back. "Because Anna told us to."

"Oi, Anna ain't in charge!" he cried, but when he saw he was being left behind, he suddenly changed his mind and took off jogging after his two companions.

The jungle was thick here, almost impenetrable, but Anna hacked wildly at it with the gun/sword, sweating and swearing as she cut much too slowly for her liking through the thick vegetation. Again, she heard the bellowing, but much closer this time. It galvanized her to work harder, faster. She sliced through some vines and spotted a large clearing up ahead, a kind of meadow that sloped gently downward toward a small lake. With a cry, she lunged that way, Syd and Adam at her heels.

As they escaped the thick of the jungle and raced down the slope, Mister and Missus emerged from behind the trees. They weren't looking their way, but at the sky instead where several pteranodon were circling. Anna saw them and ran faster than ever, Archie squealing as he glided to keep up with her. Behind them—much closer than she felt comfortable admitting—she could hear the Terror Birds squalling to one another as the hunting pack started flattening the jungle in their haste to catch up.

"Heya, heya!" she called, waving frantically to get Mister and Missus's attention. The two horned carnivores swung their enormous heads around, zeroing in on the sound of her voice.

The bigger one, Missus, made a huffing sound and turned her head so she could better focus a beady eye on Anna. Her mate followed and immediately started racing toward Anna, but Missus turned her head and rammed her small, bull-like horns into her mate's side, driving him against a tree and making it shake precariously. Mister screamed in cheated outrage.

Missus, in her greed, had done Anna a favor. She wanted Anna all to herself, the greedy sow. Swinging around, Missus opened her gigantic, slaving jaws and bellowed before charging forward. Her small red eyes looked like they were on fire.

Anna's legs turned to water and spilled her to her knees. As Missus screamed with greedy enthusiasm, she was sprayed with wind and saliva, even from a hundred yards away. Missus lowered her head and started lunging toward her, moving much faster than Anna ever imagined was possible.

Too fast. Too late. She thought these things even as Missus cracked her jaws wide open, ready to scoop up her prey. Anna only had time to throw her arms up in front of her face, for all the good that would do.

Syd suddenly appeared beside her, and, with a yell, he threw his spear as though it were a javelin. His throw was spot on. Anna watched the spear sail over her head and stick into one of Missus's eyes. Missus screamed and threw her head back. Anna tried to scramble up, but she realized her ankle was badly turned. She could feel Syd and Adam at her back, panting, their fear palatable. But they were depending on her. Depending on her plan.

"We have to keep going," she said. "Help me up."

"Yes, ma'am," Syd said, pulling Anna to her feet and supporting her under one arm.

Together, under Anna's direction, they raced right toward Missus, where she was shaking her head frantically side to side and trying to dislodge the spear. She scratched at her face, but her taloned forearms were simply too small. Mister, agitated by the whole affair, snapped at her head, further enraging her.

They were almost toe to toe with the monsters. Only at the last moment did the threesome veer off to the side and tumble into the bushes. Missus, unable to navigate correctly with the spear sticking out of one eye, and being harassed by her hungry mate, raced headlong…straight into the pack of Terror Birds emerging from the brush.

The birds, a half dozen in all, squalled and scattered, but they weren't fast enough for the giant *Carnotaurus* enlivened by pain and rage. Forgetting the spear for the moment, she turned all her hungry anger on the new foes. She stomped two or three with her bulk alone. The birds tried to regroup, but she easily tracked their movements with her one good eye, snapping at them with her huge jaws and cutting one in half with no trouble at all. She shook the remains of the bird in her teeth and dropped it to the ground before darting after the others.

The birds, confused and disoriented, turned on the larger predator and leaped at her head—one dislodging Syd's spear, which fell to the ground. Another of the birds managed to snap its jaws closed over a horn. Missus reared back with a roar, trying to shake loose her much smaller cousin. About that time, the pod of *Centrosauruses* appeared out of the woods, the big bull lowing deep in his throat at the sight of the wounded Missus. Snorting, he lowered his head and charged forward, scraping his nose horn along her lower belly.

Missus squealed and flopped to the ground, rolling around and trying to snap blindly at the bull. The giant bull grunted, shook his frilly head, and lunged again. Missus snapped her jaws over his horn. The two animals grunted and wrestled along the ground, spraying blood everywhere. The other *Centrosauruses*, most of them females, hurled themselves at Mister, driving him back with their weight and ferocity alone. One old female grunted and rammed her long horn deep into his soft, vulnerable belly, a mortal wound that left Mister howling as he toppled over.

Syd, who was lying atop Anna, rolled over and looked over his shoulder at the carnage unfolding before them. His eyes widened in appreciation, and he touched the brim of his cowboy hat. "Total chaos. Good plan."

"I wasn't really trying for a plan, and I didn't think the pod of *Centrosauruses* would get involved," Anna admitted, climbing shakily and none too steadily to her feet beside Adam.

"Thank God for gift horses," Adam said, mutilating the idiom as he watched the battle wide-eyed as the two behemoths rolled along the jungle floor, squashing the Terror Birds in their way.

He looked a little green around the gills. "Bloody hell...that is one nasty gift horse."

"Show's over," Syd said, grabbing Anna's elbow so she could lean against him for support. "Let's get the hell out of here."

| 26 |

Back to the Beginning

The air was growing hotter and more arid, and the ground gently sloping upward. Within the next couple of hours, the jungle began thinning out, and Anna knew then that they were almost to the Sonora. The animals, too, had disappeared, none wanting to venture to the edge of the unforgiving desert.

The only constant were the pteranodons, who continued to sail by overhead on updrafts of hot desert air, but even they began to thin out as Anna, Syd, and Adam limped their way out of Blood Valley. Why would they want to go near the desert? There was nothing in the desert they could subsist on, and leaving their verdant valley behind would be foolish.

Anna realized then that the whole valley was a completely self-contained ecosystem that might as well have existed at the bottom of a gigantic terrarium, cut off from the rest of the world and beholden only to its own ruthless laws.

A half hour after the last bird disappeared, the three of them began to slow as a new sound came to them—one they had never heard before.

"What is that?" Anna's ankle was still very sore, but Syd had given her one of the spears to lean on as they traveled. She kept expecting Archie to turn back at any moment and rejoin his kindred in the treetops, but he doggedly followed her, flitting from tree to tree as they struggled up a particularly daunting slope.

Adam immediately perked up. "Sounds like people."

The trio rushed to crest the slope. Just beyond the last scraggly trees, they saw it for the first time. A huge camp had been set up on the very edge of the Sonora, complete with a dozen tents, several huge cargo carts, two or three motor vehicles, and a whole corral of horses.

Anna immediately recognized Worthington and his people. They were standing around a giant bamboo cage on wheels. A *Centrosaurus* female and her young were bellowing from within the cage, which, despite its berth, was still cramping the two dinosaurs. Another similar cage held a small flock of Terror Birds that were squawking and snapping at anyone who came within five feet of their cage. A third cage stood empty. It was near this cage that Worthington and a number of his Rough Riders were gathered. They seemed to be in deep conversation over something.

"Not him," Anna said reluctantly. Her heart felt like it had dropped into the pit of her stomach. "I want to drag him into the jungle. I want to feed him to the Terror Birds..."

She was growing slowly more hysterical until Syd appeared at her side, touching her arm.

His touch seemed to calm her. "Don't. We need him to get us out of here. We don't have any decent supplies otherwise."

"But—"

"If we don't hitch a ride, we'll be stuck here forever."

"He deserves to pay, Syd! All the people he's gotten murdered..."

"Get your revenge later. It's better served cold. Trust me on that."

His words chilled her, but she knew they made good sense.

Still…

"I can't, Syd…I just can't," she sobbed. "Edmond is dead because of him. Because of bloody Carter Worthington. Edmond…and your friend Tacoma! And now he's taking those animals. Those animals don't belong to him. They don't belong to anyone!"

"I'll talk to him about the animals," Syd said softly, trying to calm her. Despite their time in the jungle, and the way it had worn them all down, he looked fit and strong, ready to take on yet another challenge. He had driven a spear into Missus's eye. Anna knew he could handle Worthington.

She sniffed and turned to Adam. With his two black eyes and various bruises, he looked as beaten and defeated as she felt. "Right, then. Off we go."

Taking her hand in his, Anna and Syd started limping toward Worthington's camp.

* * *

As the trio approached Worthington, he turned from the men he was talking to and gave them his full, undivided attention. The snake even doffed his safari hat.

"Lady Rutherford!" he said in a disgustingly jovial tone of voice and took her hand to bow over it in the English way. It was like being touched by some slimy reptile. "It's so good to finally meet you!"

Anna thought about saying a thousand things to him, some quite un-lady-like, but none seemed to encapsulate her anger. The truth was, all she wanted to do was to take her gun/sword, still tied to her side but empty of ammo, and beat him with it—use it to wipe that smug smile off his fat face.

Thankfully, Syd sensed the fission in the air, stepped in, and deftly knocked his hand away. "We need to talk, Worthington."

"Sheriff Sydney Fly! What can I do for you?" Though he was looking in Syd's general direction, Anna noticed him eyeing up Archie, perched on her shoulder, with greedy interest.

Ana reached up and put a protective hand on him.

As Syd started laying into Worthington, Anna noticed something from the corner of her eye. Adam was no longer with him. Instead, he was standing a few yards away, speaking to a slim young man that Anna recognized as Worthington's pencil-necked impresario, William Sharp. It took her a moment to remember who he was, because she almost never saw Sharp out in the sunshine. Today, though, he was glued to Worthington's side with his big ledger, making notes about the animals they were outright stealing from Blood Valley. He didn't look happy about the situation, but she saw his eyes light up when Adam approached him.

It only took a few minutes of observation for Anna to realize there was some kind of personal connection between the two men. Adam kept grabbing William's hand and babbling on about their adventures, and William kept grumbling angrily about how he'd put himself in danger. Adam's eyes lit up in a way that Anna hadn't seen since he'd talked about getting up the capital for his ranch.

Worthington was unimpressed by Syd's vitriol. Syd, now back in full sheriff mode, was laying out the charges he planned to bring against Worthington's company when they all got back to Dead Horse.

Worthington simply bit back a smile and whipped out some legal documents that (more likely than not) his no-count lawyers had drawn up to legitimize this whole sorry operation in the eyes of the State of Arizona.

"While I leave you with that to read, Sheriff, let me speak to my associate, yes? Mr. Bell!" He raised a well-manicured hand to get his man's attention.

Adam glanced up at the sound of his name, but a shadow crept behind his eyes, making him looked haunted. When he didn't immediately run to Worthington's side, Worthington went to him.

"I can't believe this," Syd said meanwhile, glancing over the documents. "He got himself licensed for this."

Anna, her hand still protectively cupped around Archie, ignored Syd's crisis and limped a few steps toward Worthington and Adam. Worthington was handing Adam a billfold, making quite a public display of it. "For your services, my friend."

Adam looked at the money like it was a snake that might bite him. It was William Sharp who took it and offered Adam a broad smile. "A down payment on the ranch. Can you believe this?" He held up the billfold in front of Adam's face. "All we need is a minor bank loan and…"

"And there is more where that came from," Worthington said, clapping him on the shoulder. "Assuming you're willing to take one more small trip back down the valley…"

"I don't know about that," Adam said in a meek but angry voice. He glanced around at the collection of caged animals. "You already have these animals. What more is there, Carter?"

"But the people don't really want these animals. They want the big ones. The dangerous ones."

"The Terror Birds are pretty bloody dangerous," Adam insisted, looking worried.

Anna managed to catch Adam's eye. She shook her head no.

Please, no…don't tell them, she silently begged, but as Worthington went on and on, singing the song of vast amounts of money, she could already see the expression changing on Adam's face. He was back on the hook, as the Americans were fond of saying.

"A *Centrosaurus*," he said suddenly. He looked away from Anna and looked at Worthington, instead. "That's what Lady Rutherford called it, anyway, and Sydney Fly wounded it. It's still stumbling around the jungle, I reckon. If I tell you where it is, how much is that worth to you, Worthington?"

Worthington only had to think about that for split seconds before saying, "Double this." He held up the billfold. "No…triple. In fact, name your price…"

Anna felt the world take a half turn around her. The caged animals. The Terror Birds nipping at their cage. And now Worthington wanted to cage the *Carnotaurus*? And then what? Drag it back to society, display it in his circus? Make money off it?

Before she even knew it, she was hurrying toward the two men. "You can't do this. You can't take that animal!" Her voice was angry and hysterical and completely fatigued. She hated the sound of it, and she probably sounded like a madwoman, but she couldn't stop herself.

She grabbed Worthington's arm and clenched it. "You cannot do this, Worthington!" she begged through a fence of teeth. "That creature doesn't belong among people!"

Worthington casually knocked her down into the dust and looked at her with such disdain, it made her skin crawl. "My dear Lady Anna, this is America, not merry ol' England. I can do anything I damned well please and the aristocracy have nothing to say about it. And what I damned well please to do is have that animal."

He turned to Adam and, a true showman, straightened his flat-brimmed hat decorated with crocodile teeth. "Mr. Bell…lead on."

Anna sat in the dust, watching the Rough Riders, Worthington, and Adam Bell arm themselves and step into the jungle. Syd came to her rescue, but the days of fatigue and dehydration were too much, and instead of picking her up, he collapsed beside her, the papers that Worthington had given him scattered around them both.

Anna started to cry.

"Fools," he whispered. "Stupid, bloody, god*damned* fools."

3

DISASTER

| 27 |

The Homecoming (II)

New York City, six months later

Anna slid another slide into the projector that Nikola Tesla had so generously donated to their cause on their arrival in New York City just the week before. "And here we see *Phorusrhacidae Brontornis*, colloquially known as the Terror Bird," she explained to the people gathered under the tent, here to see their traveling slideshow. "It was a genus of giant, flightless predatory birds that once lived in Patagonia, but my colleague Sydney Fly and I did find a lost colony in the Sonora…"

She was interrupted when a man raised his hand. "Why call them Terror Birds? Are they really terrible?"

Anna smiled appropriately to the question. "It's due to their large size and predatory nature. They were an apex predator during their time, and they still are. They belong specifically to the subfamily *Brontornithinae*, which contains extremely large and heavyset birds…"

Another hand went up. This time the man, his eyes stuck on the beautiful photographs that Syd had taken, went wide. "Is it true you and Sydney Fly fought them? What were they like? What was Dinosaur Valley like?"

Anna took a deep breath and steadied the pulse of anger pushing her to snap out something sarcastic. She didn't mind the scientific questions, but she was growing weary of people demanding all the gory details about their failed expedition.

Why am I surprised? she thought. The day she and Syd published their bestiary, the publisher had warned them that this would happen. Readers wanted sensationalism, he had said. "Terror and romance," were his exact words. They wanted to be entertained. Information was merely a side effect.

Another hand flew up. "Tell us about Archie. Is he here? Can we see him?"

She was beginning to wonder what the point of all this was.

After that traitor Adam Bell guided Worthington and his men back into the jungle, she and Syd had taken a day to sleep, eat, and refresh themselves at camp. The following day, with Worthington's party having not yet returned, Syd made the decision to go back into the jungle with his camera.

At first, Anna was reluctant. She had decided that if she never saw Blood Valley again, she would be perfectly happy, but she was also worried about Syd, and she knew he needed someone to watch his back, so she had gone, as well.

Understanding the dangers of Blood Valley much better this time, they were able to take proper precautions. Together, they took countless pictures of prehistoric animals in their natural habitat. Predators, herbivores, birds and reptiles—even the arachnids and arthropods they both hated so much. When they were done, they had so many pictures that Syd had no idea what he was going to do with them all.

During the hike back to camp, Anna suddenly blurted out, "Let's write a book about this, with your pictures. Bestiaries are awfully popular, and this will be the first of its kind anywhere. It would be educational."

Syd rubbed his chin. "But will people want to read about dinosaurs?"

"I can't speak for others, but I know I would want to read such a book. Who knows? You might make a fortune. Then you can quit being a sheriff and open a photography studio…if that's what you want."

She thought for certain that Syd was far too bull-headed to take her suggestion to heart, but while they sat in the back of a wagon as it crossed the Sonora and headed back to civilization, he suddenly blurted, "I could do it if you helped me. The bestiary, I mean. I don't know much about writin' and all that."

Anna had been sitting under a parasol, polishing her gun/sword and dreaming about ways of getting back at Worthington—and Adam, too, if possible—when his words dragged her attention around. "What? But they're *your* pictures. It should be your bestiary."

"Yeah," he agreed, lying against the buckboard, his hat pulled down against the glare of the desert sun. "But you're smart. You could help me compile them and categorize them and put the book together. I don't know the first thing."

She hadn't planned on staying in America, and she told Syd the gentlest way possible about her plans to return to her father's estate, but once they reached Dead Horse, she found a letter waiting for her at the telegraph office. It was from her father, and he was irate. He said she had ruined herself, that she was a disgrace. Her mother spent all day crying over her absence, and their friends had already begun ignoring them. He said she was as bad as Edmond, an abomination.

An abomination.

Anna spent two days locked away in her boardinghouse room, crying over that, until she realized she had nothing left to cry about. She had nothing to be ashamed of. Her parents hated her willfulness, fine. They had also hated Edmond because he was a confirmed bachelor and would never give them an heir. Their opinions meant nothing, she told herself. *Nothing.*

In any event, how could she ever return to that big, draughty house with no Edmond in it? How could she simply pick up her life and carry on like nothing had happened? Even if her parents were somehow able to look past her transgressions, in a few short years, her father the earl would have successfully buried her little adventure in the society papers. Then he would force her to marry some privileged bore, and after that, her life as she knew it would be over. She would be bent and fitted into the mold of a wife, a mother, a *Lady.* She would while her remaining life away in an estate house, dressed and coffered and crying and serving tea to the insufferable gentry she couldn't stand the sight of.

No, her life had to serve some higher purpose. Otherwise, what was the point?

"Yes," she answered breathlessly that day as she ran down Main Street to the sheriff's office to deliver her decision to Sheriff Sydney Fly in person. "I think I would very much like to write that book with you, Sheriff."

Her father thought it unseemly that a woman of her status should be staying in the colonies (and publishing a book, of all things!). In his letters, he threatened to jump the pond and drag her home by her hair, and she knew he would make good on that promise if she didn't find a solution.

But then something happened. Her mother's grief over Edmond changed everything. Once a quiet woman cowed by her husband's authority, she had intervened on Anna's part and somehow convinced her husband to let Anna remain in the colonies until she was ready to come home—but only so long as she was willing to give them frequent updates on her health and well-being and promised to keep herself professional and ladylike at all times.

As a result, Anna was seeing her mother in a new light. In fact, she was seeing herself differently, as well. In the colonies, she was an independent woman, an authoress and a scholar who was respected by her peers. The publication of their book, *Blood Valley*, quickly brought them a number of coveted accolades and the attention of some of the biggest newspapers and trade journals in America. People actually listened to her lectures on the creatures inhabiting Blood Valley—well, for the most part. In New York City, she was discovering lantern shows and cinema. There were suffragettes and street protests. It was a very progressive city, and Anna was enjoying it immensely.

Well, she enjoyed it *most* of the time.

"Lady Anna," said another man. "Can you tell us a bit more about Dinosaur Valley? Is it true that Carter Worthington, of Worthington's World of Wonders, has been stocking his collection of animals from it? Also, what do you think of his exhibit opening in one week?"

She blinked slowly at the man. She knew she was never going to get back to the scientific importance of the lecture. "Well, for one thing, it's called Dil Bii 'Ndzisgaii—Blood Valley, the ancient Navajo name for it," she answered, trying to steer the conversation away from that awful Worthington and his theatrics. "The natives knew about it for centuries before a white man ever stepped a foot there..."

"We don't want to hear about the history," a woman shouted, standing up. "Who was attacked and eaten?" The rest of the audience gasped at the woman's forward question. "Was it like in your book? Did your guide Tacoma scream when the dinosaurs ripped him apart?"

Others under the tent began shouting out questions, all of them demanding the goriest details about the mutilations and deaths that Anna and Syd had seen firsthand.

Anna, at a loss for words, was starting to feel sick. Syd, who was seated in the back of the tent, suddenly stood up. He rushed down the narrow isle and urged her to sit down in the first row while he took over the audience. In his typical perfunctory manner, he started hawking the stack of books they had brought with them.

They sold every copy, but despite their success, Anna was feeling too sick to stand up.

"I'm sorry," she said while the people filed out. She stared at her hands shaking slightly in her lap. "I thought I was stronger. I thought I could handle them, but..."

"They're asses," Syd said as he started packing up his slides and equipment. "They weren't there. They have no idea what it was really like."

He kept his head down, embarrassed and uneasy. That was her doing.

Over the past six months, she had worked very hard at keeping their relationship purely professional. She couldn't bring herself to explain her situation, the impossible standards that her parents held her to, but she had a feeling he instinctively understood the complexities of her life. There was no way she could stay in America indefinitely—and maybe not even for the foreseeable future.

Eventually, all the excitement buzzing around the book would die down, and she would need to return home.

She'd thought—hoped, really—that some American institution or university might pop up, courting her for an internship. Then she would have a reason to stay forever. She hoped her celebrity status would be a boon. But, so far, no one was knocking on her door.

She was still only a woman, she had to remind herself. Even in a place as progressive as America, she was merely Syd's "attractive sidekick," as their publisher insisted on referring to her. An appendage. Women didn't become archaeologists or professors. They didn't work on staff at university. They didn't have careers.

She started to say something when the sound of clapping interrupted her thoughts. Turning, she noticed a tall, imposing gentleman of middle age walking down the aisle toward them. He was dressed smartly in a dark suit, but there was a grimness about him, like someone who might have been an undertaker in another life.

"That was quite a performance," he said jovially, stopping a few feet away from them. Despite his outward friendly manner, there was something about him that immediately rubbed Anna the wrong way. He looked sly and slick, and he reminded her of Worthington in some way—a man who knew what he wanted and did whatever was necessary to get it.

He pulled back his coat to reveal a badge. "My name is Reginald King. Agent Reginald King. I'm with the Pinkertons."

Syd immediately stiffened. "I assure you we have the license to speak here..."

Agent King waved it away. "That's not why I'm here." He paused and eyed them both carefully up and down, with a policeman's strict attention to detail. "You two are the dinosaur people. Is it true, everything you wrote about in the book?"

He picked up the battered hardcopy that Anna and Syd used as a reference and paged through it quickly. "The Terror Birds and the one-eyed *Carnotaurus*?"

Anna stepped up to match Agent King's question. In general, she took care of all business related to the bestiary. "It is. What can we do for you, Agent? Why are you here?"

He stopped on the pages containing the photographs of the Terror Birds. Just the sight of them still brought a shiver to Anna's shoulders. "I'm actually here because of something only tangibly related to your adventures in Blood Valley. You never say as much in your book, but as I understand it, whilst in the valley, you were not alone. There was another man with you?"

"Adam Bell," Anna said quickly. "Yes, but I would hardly call him a man. We had no real association, and he turned out to be a traitor." Her voice sounded embittered by just the mention of Adam Bell—a man she pitied as much as she despised. For one moment in time, Anna thought she and Adam had had some kind of connection, but she'd been wrong. Adam only loved the money that Worthington could offer.

Agent King nodded. "You are aware of his reputation? His crimes as a rustler and bootlegger?"

Anna didn't immediately answer. She knew enough about Adam that she didn't want to be associated with his reputation. The papers called him "Bootleg" Bell. He was notorious for fencing rare valuables and trafficking in stolen merchandise and animals, among other crimes. But because he moved around with Worthington's traveling show, the law couldn't serve any warrants on him. He was never in one place long enough for them to catch him—not that he was easy to catch, anyway. The man was as slippery as an eel.

She crossed her arms across the bodice of her gown. "I know the man is a thief and a general rapscallion. We call him a 'gentleman thief' in London, but he's hardly a gentleman."

Agent King nodded. "I've been tracking his exploits for years. I even caught up to him at one point in El Paso, but he managed to escape." King paused and his eyes turned dark. His good humor seemed to slip, and Anna caught a glimpse of a frustrated and obsessive policeman beneath his smile. "I mean to bring him to heel once and for all."

"Understandable, Agent King. But I don't see what any of that has to do with us."

Agent King withdrew a flier from his pocket. It was an advertisement for Worthington's World of Wonders. Anna took it from the man and examined it. It was for the new exhibit, the one opening soon. At the center of the collage of lurid and sensational images was the dreadful Missus, jaws wide open as if to swallow the reader, with the Terror Birds and other prehistoric creatures surrounding her. Before Anna could ask any questions, King filled her in on the details.

"Worthington's new exhibit is opening in just one week's time. That means that that devil Adam Bell will be here. I mean to capture him, but I may need some help."

"I don't understand, Agent King." She tried to hand back the poster. Syd was a lawman, but Anna knew absolutely nothing about police work.

"I need someone who can get close to him. Someone who can pin him down long enough for my men to move in."

Syd stepped up, glowering, and took the flier from Anna's hand. He examined the details as Anna had, and Anna saw him shake his head, which surprised her. She knew he was far from fond of Adam. She would have thought he'd relish the chance to bring him to heel.

"What's in it for us? You realize you are getting us in the middle of our book tour?"

Agent King glanced around the sad little tent. "Yes, well, if you want to call this…horse and pony show…a tour."

Anna felt her hackles go up, and she knew then that she was right about Agent King. He was the type of man who would sell his own mother up a river just to get the accolades associated with capturing a man like Adam "Bootleg" Bell.

He offered them a shrewd look before turning to Anna with a little smiling ticking the corner of his face. "The Pinkertons have connections, Lady Rutherford. Military. Government. How does a tour of the biggest universities across this great nation sound to you two young people?"

He paused to let that sink in. "You help me get that scoundrel Bell, and I promise you will be the most popular authors in the United States…indeed, the world."

| **28** |

Blood Money

"**A**dam, stop fretting," William said, standing at the full-length mirror in their caravan and fixing his bowtie. "Everything will be fine."

Adam lay sprawled in bed, eyes closed, listening to William banging about the caravan as he got his cufflinks on and his suit jacket over his waistcoat. Each thud made his head throb and his body wince in response, the end result of too much rotgut the night before.

From outside came the low hum of human activity as Worthington's men set up the exhibits. The pounding of hammers and the shouting of men made him grimace. Beyond that came the busy bustle of the New York streets: coaches, horse-drawn carts, backfiring flivvers. Human activity. Human life. Normally, Worthington preferred the remote southwestern circuit, but the new exhibit was hitting all the major eastern seaboard cities, which is why they were here in Coney Island for the week.

He hated the bloody city. In too many ways, it reminded him of the East End, and that was something he could do without, thank you very bloody much.

William, who hailed from this town, thought it was all quite grand. He talked about the operas and theaters with great enthusiasm. He was also the bouncy morning type, always the first out of bed and the first dressed in his bloody manic, pencil-necked way. He also drank like a fish and seemed capable of neutralizing alcohol faster than a Scottish seaman. It was downright inhuman.

Sighing, Adam pulled the sheets up over his head to block out the blinding morning sunlight.

William went to the bed and jerked the sheet away. "Get up," he said in a disgustingly chipper tone of voice. "We're going to be late!"

"*You're* going to be late. Worthington has a whole new police detail because of that one-eyed monster. The wanker doesn't need me." Adam grabbed the sheet and petulantly pulled it over his face again, trying to muffle the thunderous noises outside that threatened to make his head explode like a watermelon being shot up in the Wild West exhibit.

"Is that what you're worried about? The flatfoots?"

"I'm a wanted man, Will."

"Those Micks are so stupid, they don't even know who you are, and even if they did, Worthington took care of that for you, remember?"

Adam moaned.

William huffed. "Fine. You want to be a child, be a child. I plan to work opening night and make us some bank." William paused for effect. "You know…M-O-N-E-Y? For the ranch?"

After their return from Blood Valley, everything had gone back to normal in a truly surreal fashion. Worthington went back to frantically designing whole new exhibits around his shiny collection of prehistoric animals. William picked up the pen and began cooking the books like a madman. And Adam went back to head of security—a job he loathed and had never really wanted anyway.

He could think of no job more distasteful than wandering around the fairgrounds, threatening kids who were trying to sneak in for free. If he'd had his way, he would have left long ago, but he couldn't seem to convince William to give it up already and come away with him to the western frontier.

Everything was different for Adam. Everything was changed. And yet nothing had changed at all.

"We *have* money for the ranch," Adam growled from beneath the sheet. *Blood money*, he silently added as he ran a quick tally in his head of how many people Worthington had sacrificed to expand his traveling show. "A lot of money!"

"You're not the money guy, Adam. You just don't get it."

Suddenly enraged, Adam sat up and shoved the sheet away, glaring up at William. "Why do we need *more* money? Christ, Will, it's been six bloody months..." He stopped and touched his head, berating himself from raising his voice above a graveyard whisper.

"Two words: backup revenue." William raised two fingers in the air for emphasis. He gave Adam a shrewd look that turned his eyes to glimmering black beads and made his lips stretch into a wolfish half-smile. "Look, you don't understand money. I do. We need at least a year's worth of capital before we even invest in the event it all goes sideways..."

"Why would the ranch go sideways?" Adam gave William a shrewd look right back. He might not understand the ins and outs of capital investments the way William did, but he knew when he was being played.

William was stalling. Adam just didn't understand why.

No, that wasn't true. He knew.

William Sharp was a greedy man. It was one of the things that had attracted Adam to him in the first place. But enough was enough. They had more than enough to leave Worthington's freak show in the dust—and the sooner, the better, as far as Adam was concerned. They had been here a week; if the show continued apace, that meant staying another week, and that made Adam just a little bit nervous with all the Micks crawling around.

Sighing with exasperation, William sat down on the edge of the bed and took Adam's hand in a sign of solidarity. "Look, darling, I know what you've been through. The way you tell it, it's like I was there in Blood Valley with you..."

"You weren't there!" Adam snapped and jerked his hand away as a thousand bloody images fluttered through his mind like one of those fancy newsreels at the moving pictures. "You have no idea what it was like. You never will..."

William crinkled up his long nose in response. "That may be so, but keep in mind, everything I'm doing, I'm doing for us. We're in this together, Adam. We always were."

Are you? Adam wondered. *Are you in it for us...or only the money?* He knew the siren-call of cold, hard cash all too well.

When Adam didn't immediately respond, William leaned down and brushed a brief kiss across Adam's lips. That old tingle remained between them, but now it was tempered with concern. For himself. For them. Hell, for the bloody marks coming to see the show tonight.

Adam bloody hated what that old bastard Worthington was doing. The animals in his show were wild, uncontrollable. He'd seen them up close and personal, and he was one of the few men to walk away from the situation.

He's just courting disaster, he though, not for the first time. Worthington...that greedy, stupid, bloody fool...

He thought back to Blood Valley as he often did, but inevitably his thoughts circled around to Lady Anna and that look she had given him when they'd parted company. He kept telling himself she was a stuck-up, high-class chit who knew nothing about struggling to make ends meet. How could she? She was one of *them*. One of the Four Hundred. Never had to work a day in her whole bloody life. No worries. Everything given to her on a silver platter. But he just kept coming around to her expression that last day on the edge of Blood Valley. Her disappointment. Not anger or rage. *Disappointment.* She had expected him to leave the one-eyed *Carnotaurus* in the jungle like it was some kind of wounded, defenseless animal.

What the hell was wrong with him of late? William was right, as usual. Money was good. The more money, the better. How else were they ever going to make lives for themselves out west on the frontier? Not the bloody old-fashioned way, that was for certain. This was about them, about William and him, he reminded himself.

Rubbing his bleary eyes, his elbow knocked the empty whiskey bottle to the floor, where it rolled away in a half circle before coming to a stop and dripping its last contents onto the scuffed floorboards of the caravan where he and William had been living rough for the past five years.

Grinning his greedy grin, William slapped Adam's cheek. "Get your lazy, British, drunken ass out of bed and help me. We have a show to put on, darling, and money to make!"

| 29 |

The Greatest Show on Earth

The fairgrounds were vast. It was obvious that Worthington had leased far more space than he usually did for his traveling exhibit. It stretched over most of Coney Island's Steeplechase Park, confiscating almost every square inch that was not already occupied by rides or tents, including the mechanical horse race course that the park was named for and the scale models of the Eiffel Tower and Big Ben. A huge, fire-engine-red banner had been erected over the arching gates, and it read: WORTHINGTON'S WORLD OF PREHISTORIC WONDERS. Along both sides of the gate were paintings of the new exhibits snarling in their cages.

As Anna walked arm-in-arm with Syd through the gates, Archie fluttering behind them, she felt a bone-deep chill at the luridly painted posters. She refocused her attention on the banner. "He changed the name of his exhibit."

Syd's mustache quirked up on one side. "Did you think he wouldn't?"

"I think he's an arrogant fool who is going to get someone hurt. Someone other than himself, of course."

Archie alighted on her shoulder and hid behind her ear, the crowd of people making him too nervous to show his face.

They started down the enormous pavilion, which was crammed with people—visitors, vendors, barkers, and police—not that they would be much help if one of the animals got loose, Anna reflected. Along with the local establishments lining both sides, Anna noticed that Worthington's usual collection of animals were on display first —lions, tigers, pandas, elephants, giraffes, even kangaroos and other marsupials from Australia. Each had its own small alcove with a barker explaining the different habits of the animals inside. Most of the animals looked miserable and bored.

Anna and Syd stopped by the orangutan display and looked in at a pair of animals clustered together on a branch, furiously eating nuts and throwing shells at passersby. Anna almost laughed. That was exactly how she felt about Worthington's show.

They had their choice of alcoves, if they wanted them. Despite the crowded pavilion, and the fact that Worthington had made his fortune on showing off these animals to anyone willing to pay the admission fee, almost no one was interested in the more mundane creatures—the ones they could see anytime. In the new world, where everyone knew about Blood Valley, these animals had become boring and maybe even obsolete. Instead, everyone was rushing toward the special exhibits at the far end of the park.

Syd, standing beside Anna and getting sprayed with shells, turned to her and said, "Are you ready?"

Anna let out a breath and glanced around at the other finely dressed men and women promenading around them, most headed toward the new exhibits. "I don't know, Syd. I don't like the way this feels."

"I know what you mean," he said, but it obviously didn't bother him the way it did her. He turned and pretended to read the big plaque on the orangutan exhibit. "Adam is a criminal. As such, he deserves to be brought to justice. Besides…"

Anna waved it away. "Yes, yes, I know what he did…but it still feels wrong. Dirty, I mean. I don't play dirty, Sydney Fly. I never have." She swallowed hard and looked up into his piercing blue eyes.

Did he think her very naïve? Probably, but she had never been asked to do something like this before, to be this crafty and under-handed. She didn't like the way it made her feel. "I don't like what he's done, of course, but I understand why he does it. I knew men like him back in London. They would do almost anything to get ahead…"

"He burned our camp, Anna. He helped drag that monster back to civilization."

"I know." She swallowed and reached up to cup a hand protec-tively around Archie. "But they weren't things done out of malice. It was desperation. Adam is a desperate man."

"He's a criminal," Syd groused, looking away at a vast cage full of colorful macaws. "If he wants a better life, a different life, he should work for it like everyone else, not just take what he thinks he's owed."

Anna was silent in response to that. She recalled the exchange between Adam Bell and William Sharp. London was replete with Adam's kind. There were even special clubs set up to protect the anonymity of its members. Her father didn't know she knew about such things, but Anna wasn't so naïve as to not understand the private nature of her own twin brother. She knew why her father had turned his back on him, but it had never made her love him any less, despite all the duplicity of his life. But, to her father, he had been an abomination.

She wanted to convey all this to Syd, but she didn't know how he would react. "Adam is different, Syd. His is in a different situation."

"Aren't we all?" Syd snapped his attention back around to Anna. His face was hard as stone and his eyes glimmered like sharp flint. "How does he have any more right to do the things he does than anyone else?"

She didn't know how to answer him and stuttered on some kind of response.

His anger immediately cooled and he put his hand gently on her wrist, his form of an apology. "Sorry. All this is as uncomfortable to me as it is to you. Do you want me to go alone? I can handle this situation just fine..."

"Absolutely not!" Anna blew out her breath in exasperation. There was no way she was being left behind. "Besides, he'll take one look at you and run for the hills."

She took a gulp of air before continuing. "I'm just saying...let's keep an open mind. I don't know that I trust Agent Reginald King."

Syd nodded. "Too ambitious. Obsessed. I get you." He pushed his cowboy hat back on his head and thought a long moment. "But what about his promise of connections?"

Anna had been rolling that around her head for days. Was turning Adam in worth a chance to speak at a university that probably wouldn't want to listen to her anyway? Or just wanted all the gory details of their expedition to Blood Valley?

"Tell you what," Syd said, interrupting her thoughts. "We'll take Adam somewhere private and talk to him. If things don't seem right, we'll decide what to do then."

Anna smiled at that, grateful for Syd's understanding and flexibility. "Really? Do you mean that?"

Syd tucked one hand behind his back and bent over her hand in the gentlemanly fashion. He looked like some cowboy version of a dashing hero in a book of romance. "Anything for you, Lady Anna."

She threw herself on him and kissed the scruffy side of his cheek, despite passersby giving her a slightly shocked look at her forward behavior. At the same time, Archie squalled and jumped up into the air.

"Thank you, Syd!" She swore she could see him turning beat red from her kiss, but chose not to mention it. Linking her arm through his, she led him toward the new part of the exhibit while Archie trailed behind them, warbling at all the exciting things to see.

A full-sized coliseum had been erected, the same one that Worthington normally used for his trick riders and animal tamers, but posters covered the wall, advertising the prehistoric exhibits one could witness for "only one dollar apiece." Anna couldn't believe the price he was commanding—more than ten times a normal exhibit in this city!

After the ticket master took their money, they were given a stub and told to follow the ascending staircase to the top of the coliseum, which was packed solid with people. There wasn't a seat to be had and it was standing room only. Anna thought that maybe every person in New York City was here today.

Even standing at the top of the coliseum, it was difficult to see past the wall of gawkers blocking the show down below. A vendor was running about, selling opera glasses to better see at a distance, but Anna was so short that she knew it would make no difference. Syd, however, was tall, and not at all proud. Like when they were underground in the rocky cavern system, he made a saddle of his hands and jerked his head toward the show.

"Ladies first."

"Why thank you, Sheriff." Anna slid the toe of her walking boot into his hands and he bumped her up so she was sitting on his shoulder, her arm curled around his neck for balance. That put her well above everyone else, with the exception of Archie (who hovered above her, having the best seat in the house), and within easy sight of the show. She gasped at the sight.

There were no bars, nothing to separate the animals from the audience. Much like in Barnum & Bailey's affair, there were several rings—four to be exact. In the first ring, the juvenile *Centrosaurus* raced rambunctiously around with a cowboy sitting in a custom saddle on his back, riding him like a bull and shouting at the crowd while rodeo clowns threw confetti into the juvenile's face. It was obvious the animal was still half-wild, and the loud noises and confetti only made him wilder still as he ran and bucked in circles. The crowd laughed at the juvenile's energy, but to see a proud, prehistoric beast like this being manipulated like it was a common bovine made Anna sick. Its scaly skin shone and it lowed and barked as it raced in figure eights, driven on by the rider on its back driving his spurs into its sides. The more she watched, the more horrible it became, though the gawkers seemed to like it, especially the children.

The second attraction was even more elaborate than the first. In this ring, a beautiful trick rider in a sequenced leotard was using her whips and crop to put the sad-looking mother *Centrosaurus* through her paces. Decorated in a glittery circus caparison, she trotted in a circle, so large a beast she was able to balance an African elephant on her back, which then had another trick rider doing stunts atop the elephant. Even though she followed the directions of her handler, the *Centrosaurus* lowed pathetically while the ringmaster stood to one side, going on at length about the animal, its environment and behavior—most of which he got hideously wrong anyway.

The barker talked, the people laughed. The animal lowed.

The third ring had the big, wounded bull from Blood Valley, the one Missus had fought. He was alive, but quite scarred from the battle. Too wild to perform, he was chained down, though he did everything in his power to pull at his binds, and when he did, the people screamed in response. Anna wondered what his purpose here was, then the ringmaster chilled her blood by announcing that that night, the bull would be battling his arch-nemesis for the pleasure of the crowd. They only had to return at nine o'clock. She had a pretty good idea of who that was—and Missus's conspicuous lack of presence only convinced her further.

"This is barbaric," Syd said, and his words surprised her. They mirrored her thoughts exactly, but she hadn't expected to hear the words from his lips.

The fourth ring was the only one containing what looked like a gigantic birdcage. Inside were several Terror Birds hissing and ramming the bars. They looked thin and malnourished, and their heads were bloodied from their constant assaults. An animal tamer, not brave enough to go inside the cage, was whipping them back and trying to speak, but they screeched so loudly that people periodically gasped, and she heard several children start to cry.

Anna felt a lump forming in her throat. Despite the fact that these were the creatures responsible for Edmond's death, she still managed to feel appalled by it all. "Look at them. This has to stop," she said. "That fool Worthington will keep at it until they've broken through."

"I know," said Syd. For once, he looked truly concerned as one of the Terror Birds rammed the bars of the cage for what had to be the hundredth time, rattling it concerningly.

She tapped Syd on the shoulder. "Let me down, please." She pushed a few errant blonde curls out of her face. "I don't want to see this. Let's move on."

Syd did not argue.

Down on the pavilion once more, Anna stopped and pointed. "Syd, look."

Adam Bell was sitting on the dusty ground in the narrow alley between a tobacco shop and an apothecary selling cure-alls. The wall he was sprawled against had a huge advertisement for Dr.

Pepper's Pepsin Bitters, but it was a bottle of cheap bourbon that he was drinking from.

Not waiting for a response, she grabbed Syd's hand and started dragging him that way. "Adam…Adam!" She waved frantically.

Adam Bell slowly stood up, the bottle of rotgut dangling from his hand, then glanced around like he was preparing to make a break for it.

"Adam, wait!" She glanced both ways across the pavilion as they crossed it, but she didn't see Agent King anywhere, or any other police officers. The coast looked clear. "Stop! We need to talk. It's important! It's about your safety!"

"Anna!" Syd barked as she dragged him along. He just narrowly missed smacking into a couple crossing the pavilion as he struggled to keep his cowboy hat on. "Anna, dammit…we said we would talk about this!"

"We did! We talked and we both agreed."

"No, we did not!"

Anna skidded to a halt as they reached him. Reaching out, she grabbed Adam's sleeve and jerked on it, making the man start like she had slapped him. "You have to get out of here, now! The Pinkertons are looking for you!"

"Oh, for heaven's sake…"

Anna ignored Syd's complaint. "A man by the name of Agent Reginald King came to speak with us. He wants us to get you somewhere where his agents can collar you. He's probably not very far, so you absolutely must get out of here now!"

Adam just looked annoyed and ripped his sleeve loose. "What the bloody hell are you going on about, you crazy chit!"

"The Pinkertons!" Anna huffed with exasperation. "Agent King said you were wanted in several states!"

Adam frowned at that, but then looked around the fairgrounds like someone was going to ambush him at any moment. "That's impossible. I did some stuff, aye, but it was under Worthington's orders. He had all that sorted."

"Are you sure?" Syd asked with an upraised eyebrow. "This is Worthington we're talking about."

Adam stiffened. "Oi! It was part of our deal. I bring him the dinosaurs and he gets all the charges dropped…"

Gradually, he stiffened as his eyes traveled beyond the two of them and centered on something suspicious at a distance. "No…bloody hell!" He turned and punched the wall of the apothecary hard enough to make him wince and to rattle the whole wooden structure.

Anna and Syd turned in time to spot a couple of men in formal black coats heading down the pavilion. One of them was Agent Reginald King. She wondered if it was possible Agent King had had her and Syd followed. She wouldn't put it past the man.

"Well, you just became expendable to Worthington," Anna said. "Much like the rest of us."

Adam let out a string of curses and smashed his half-empty bottle on the ground.

Anna put both hands up. "Let us help you."

"We are *not* helping him escape the Pinkertons!" Syd stated.

"Fine." She threw Syd a cold look before returning her full attention to Adam. "Let *me* help you…"

Adam jerked away from both of them. He stumbled, quite obviously drunk, and almost fell against a nearby rain barrel. "I don't need neither of you wankers. I'll manage just fine, thanks bloody much!"

Sighing, Anna stepped back. "Fine. Then we'll create a distraction while you get away."

"Anna…" Syd began, but Anna was determined, and she had her own mind. Willfulness, her father called it.

Turning around, she ran back toward the coliseum. When she got close enough to the next group of people heading up the staircase to the top, she let out a bloodcurdling scream and dropped to the ground in what she felt was quite a dramatic swoon.

It had the desired effect. Everyone in the immediate vicinity turned their attention on the fainted female in front of the lurid coliseum posters. Syd raced up to her and knelt down. "Anna!"

She peeked one eye open, then winked at him. Soon enough, people began to gather, including Agent King and his friend.

"What in tarnation is going on?" Agent King demanded to know. "Lady Anna Rutherford? What's happened to her?"

Syd, catching on, looked up, putting on a distressed face. "Agent King, the sight of the dinosaurs made Lady Anna faint!"

"The...?" He looked confused, then seemed to catch on and looked around.

But by then, Adam was long gone.

| 30 |

Under Fire

"**W**ill!" Adam yelled, banging through the door of the accounting caravan. "Will, we have to get out of here…!"

William Sharp was, thankfully, fatally predictable. Adam knew he would be right there in the Box Office Trailer, working the books as always. He almost never left during a workday. He even had one of Worthington's work hands bring him his meals. So it came as something of a shock when Adam stepped inside the narrow space and saw it was empty.

William's desk and chair were there, but William was nowhere to be found.

"Will! William, where the bloody hell are you?"

No answer.

A thought occurred to Adam. He went do Will's desk, but the cash box was missing, along with his ledgers. Adam couldn't understand why the cash box would be missing with all the cash from today's ticket sales, except that maybe William had cleared out suddenly. Maybe the Pinkertons had leaned on him?

"No…"

Banging back through the door, Adam nearly fell down the stairs to the gravel lot behind Steeplechase Park where the owner, George Tilyou, let Worthington's staff set up camp. Worthington's show was huge and required over a thousand men to move from city to city—mostly carnies, unemployed laborers, and criminals on the run like himself. As a result, their camp sprawled for nearly a quarter of a mile, made up of hundreds of caravans and innumerable tents set up for such basic amenities as cooking, bathing, and other daily activities. It was colloquially referred to by the men as Tent City, and it looked it, too.

Off to one side, near Worthington's posh caravan, was the big top, a huge, four-story tent that was chained off from the rest of the lot and which bore multiple Keep Out signs for the sake of the public—the place where Worthington kept his star performers.

Adam, stumbling down the stairs, caught himself at the last second and then hurried across the lot, past the big top, toiletry tents, and mess hall, to the private trailer that he and William shared. He scrambled up the stairs and threw the door open...and stopped.

William was sitting in a chair by their bed, looking petrified. Worthington, meanwhile, was ripping their caravan apart, throwing boxes, linens, and their clothes around willy-nilly, a disgruntled look on his face.

"Where is it, William, you worthless little queen?" Worthington growled, sounding enraged. "Tell me!"

William, pale and sweating, just looked at Adam, and in that moment, Adam understood. Worthington knew. Somehow, he *knew.*

Adam had never seen the normally cool and collected Worthington in such a state of rage. The man stood up and with a roar kicked one of their boxes of books and trinkets across the caravan. The box spilled over, dumping their collective possessions onto the floor.

He turned to Adam, and Adam saw the pistol in Worthington's hand. "You! Close the door. Now."

"The hell's going on?"

"I said close the door," Worthington said coldly.

With a gun trained on him, Adam realized he had no choice. He closed it, plunging the room into near darkness. Most of the men who worked for Worthington shared their space—two to a caravan, was the general rule—but in Adam and William's case, they usually papered the windows to keep nosy passersby away. They had had to do so after Worthington caught them in bed one night. As a result, it was darker than usual.

Worthington indicated the desk with the glimmering nose of the gun. "Light the lamp, you traitorous bastard."

Adam felt his stomach lurch and then fall, along with all of their dreams. He contemplated diving for the gun and wresting it away, but Worthington knew him too well, and in three steps, he was standing beside William's chair. He grabbed William by his oiled hair and jerked his head to one side, sticking the nose of the gun into his temple.

Worthington chambered a round causing William to whimper. "Still want to do it?"

Adam stiffened. Worthington smiled, his teeth gleaming like ceramic in the dark. "I said light the lamp, Bell, before I blow your man's brains out his damn ears."

Adam had to make a conscious decision to calm himself. If he acted rashly, he'd get William killed. He'd get them both killed.

He went about the little ritual of lighting their lone oil lamp. Soon enough, yellow light fluttered across the walls of the cramped little caravan like moth wings, illuminating William's old tintypes on the walls, the posters they had collected, and, of course, William's pale, frightened face. As criminals went, William was strictly small-time, white-collar, and generally frightened of his own shadow. He couldn't even kill the spiders that made their way inside the caravan. After replacing the glass chimney and ball shade, Adam turned back to Worthington with a stony expression.

"Is it true?" he asked Worthington. "Did you sell me out to the Pinkertons?"

Worthington looked momentarily surprised. "How do you know anything about that?"

"Well, that answers my question," Adam growled low. "Who's the traitorous bastard now, Worthington?"

Worthington ignored him. "I want my money, Bell. All of it. Did you honestly think I wouldn't notice?" He shook William by the hair, making him flinch. "Monkey boy here was sloppy and greedy. Ten thousand. Did you honestly think I wouldn't notice that kind of money gone missing?"

Adam thought for a second. "Yeah, we played each other." He raised his hands so Worthington didn't freak out and do anything stupid. "But let Will go, Worthington. The embezzlement was my idea, not his. Will was just doing what I told him to do."

Worthington laughed at that. "Really, Bell?" He sounded far from convinced, and the man's eyes never left him. His anger was palatable even though he smiled the smile of a true showman. He would have made P.T. Barnum proud. "You disappoint me. You grew up in a workhouse, didn't you?"

Adam frowned but kept his hands up. "What has that got to do with anything?"

"Do you honestly think I would believe such a flimsy lie? *Your* idea?"

Again, Worthington laughed. "Bell, you're an illiterate cur. You couldn't embezzle your way out of a paper sack. Now, where the hell is my money? Where did this little punk hide it?" He jabbed William in the ear, making him squeak in fear.

Adam seethed. All the things he had done for Worthington…all the bloody shite he had put up with in Blood Valley…and now the Pinkertons…and the man was worried about ten thousand measly dollars they had hidden under the floorboards?

Unable to control himself, Adam flung himself at Worthington with a roar of rage.

The assault was so sudden that Worthington did absolutely nothing as Adam connected with the big man. The force of the impact drove Worthington to the floor with Adam on top. Roaring uncontrollably, Adam grabbed Worthington's gun hand and smashed it repeatedly against the floor until he released the weapon and it skittered away. After that, he started laying into Worthington, boxing his face over and over, putting every bit of his insult and frustration into it.

Worthington grunted at each impact, and each time, his face became a bigger platter of blood pudding. Adam was actually enjoying himself until a book came out of nowhere—one that Worthington had been able to grab from the fallen box—and smashed him across the face. The impact knocked him off the man.

Adam, moaning through a broken nose, scrambled to find his bearings and his feet, but by the time he was standing, so was Worthington. His face was a bloody ruin…but he had the gun in his hand once more.

"You little worthless punk," Worthington growled through the blood on his mouth. He extended his arm, taking a bead on Adam's chest.

Adam knew it was too late. No escape for him this time. No clever getaways. He even closed his eyes and, a second later, heard the explosive bang of the gun…but though he was knocked to the floor, there was no burning pain in his chest.

Opening his eyes, he realized that Will had moved from his seat. He'd thrown himself against Adam at the last moment.

Now, William Sharp stood weaving on his feet while a large blossom of blood bloomed over his heart. He even touched the wound, his eyes full of surprise.

"Will? Will!" Adam grabbed the man by the shoulders as he dropped to the floor and rolled him over.

William stared up at him, smiling. His glasses were crooked and there were bubbles of blood on his lips. The patch of red was growing larger very quickly across the front of Will's gold brocade waistcoat, and more shiny red was gathering in a puddle underneath him. William raised his head slightly and said in his very posh and straight-laced voice, "Killed the spider this time…"

"Will," said Adam, struggling to hold his dead weight close. "Will?"

William stiffened, shuddered, and went limp in Adam's arms. A drop of blood fell to the floorboards from his slightly open mouth, and then the light went out of his eyes forever.

Slowly, ever so slowly, Adam lowered the man to the floor. He stared at him a long, hard moment before turning his attention on Worthington, standing near the table where the lamp was flickering.

"You…you…" Adam wheezed. His voice was barely human, nearly inaudible, and he kept gulping to keep himself from screaming. He knew if he started screaming, he wouldn't be able to stop.

Before he even knew what he was doing, he'd run to the wall where he kept his crossbow mounted and yanked it down. The quiver came with it, spilling bolts all over the floor like pickup sticks, but he managed to grab up a handful, though he had no idea what he was going to do with them.

Worthington's eyes went wide. He knew that in these close quarters, Adam couldn't miss. He was a dead man. Turning, he grabbed the oil lamp and, with a shout, flung it at Adam. It narrowly missed colliding with Adam's shoulder. Instead, the lamp hit the floor under the drapes, the glass shattering. The drapes were instantly engulfed in flames. Second later, the entire window was burning as the dry, decades-old wood of the caravan fed the ravenous flames.

Adam didn't see. Didn't care. Let it burn, he thought. The caravan, the money under the floorboards, their life together, his and William's. Let it all burn. Let it bloody burn!

"Worthington!" he finally screamed through tears of rage as he struggled to prime a bolt in the crossbow.

Worthington all but fell backward out of the trailer.

Crossbow finally primed, Adam followed.

| 31 |

Fire in the Hole

The emergency team from the ambulance coach was busy trying to revive Anna from her "swoon" when she heard the sudden screams from the far corner of the fairgrounds. She opened first one eye, then both, then sat bolt upright while the medic working over her with smelling salts started in response.

"Syd!" she shouted. "What was that?"

Syd, hovering on the edges of the crowd, turned to look in the direction of the scream. The Pinkertons turned in that direction, as well. Agent King even reached for his gun. Seconds later, a small crowd of people scurried past, shouting about something or other, though their voices were a jumble and she had no idea what they were saying. Shortly after that, Anna smelled the acrid stench of smoke for the first time.

"Fire," said Anna, springing to her feet and pushing the medic away. "Do you smell it?"

"Hell, yeah." Syd's attention was riveted to the area where the people had emerged. In their elaborate costumes, they looked like employees, vendors, hucksters, and performers. Distantly, Anna saw a small collection of caravans, most with Worthington's World of Wonders logo painted on them…and a billow of smoke rising above them as they collectively burned.

Anna clapped a hand over her mouth. "Dear God, the fairgrounds are on fire." She grabbed Syd by the arm. "Do you think Adam is all right?"

Syd scrunched up his face. "I think Adam can take care of himself."

Ignoring Syd's comment, Anna checked the handy gun/sword she had stowed away under her coat. Since returning from Blood Valley, she took it everywhere with her, though she knew that was probably silly. Somehow, though, it made her feel better to know it was there. It was right where she'd left it, polished and loaded, ready to use…if worst came to worst.

Syd didn't understand, of course, but she absolutely had to help Adam if he'd gotten himself into trouble. Maybe he didn't want her help, but she had a feeling that he needed it. She didn't think anyone had ever helped him in the entirety of his life.

She pointed. "I'm headed that way to look for him."

She tried to take off toward the burning caravans, but Syd grabbed her by the wrist, halting her momentum. "Anna, I really don't think…" he began, and she threw him a look that said it all. He wasn't going to win this war, or any war with her.

Sighing, he let her go. "Fine," he said, checking his own rig, "But I'm coming with you."

* * *

Adam squeezed off several bolts at once in Worthington's general direction, but the man was faster than he'd ever anticipated, and he kept zigzagging across the gravel lot of Tent City. Within seconds, Worthington had disappeared into the vast labyrinth of caravans and tents.

Swearing and sweating, Adam turned back to the caravan he and William had shared for years. This time, Adam let out a frustrated howl as he watched the flames springing up and consuming everything in their trailer. The dry wood, the drapes and clothes...all of it fed the flames and created a wall of heat like a blast furnace.

He quickly scurried up the steps, his heart knocking, blood pumping, hoping to retrieve William's body from the fire, but a wall of smoke and flames jumped up, preventing him from ducking inside. In minutes, the air had turned to a lethal burning fog. His eyes burned too badly, and each breath of the smoke-infused air made it feel like he had saws cutting away at his lungs. Cursing and sputtering, he backed down the stairs to the gravel lot, the crossbow sagging in one hand.

That's when he noticed the flames had eaten their way through the mean tin roof, collapsing it, and now, it was jumping to the next caravan, which was parked less than a couple of feet away. He knew the women who lived there; they were the Sanderson Sisters, trick riders who rode the elephants in Worthington's show. He and William had been good friends with them, because unlike what the rest of the world wanted to see, the two girls who lived together weren't sisters at all.

He looked once more on his and William's trailer—all the two of them had built together—but now the smoke was such that he could no longer see much. The whole thing was collapsing inward and William's body was lost. But the Sanderson Sisters—they he might still save.

Racing up the steps, he pounded frantically on the door until one of the girls, Starry, opened it. Half-clothed, she immediately saw the flames and started to scream for her lover to grab as many of their belongings as she could.

"Warn the others," Adam said. "Warn as many people as you can!!"

Starry nodded her head.

Adam, meanwhile, moved to the next trailer, and then the next. In Tent City, word traveled fast. Within minutes, most of the employees were standing on the gravel in various states of undress, clutching their meager belongings, crying or screaming, or vainly trying to get water into buckets to douse the flames from the bath tents.

Despite Adam's attempts at helping, the water wasn't coming nearly fast enough, and the collection of caravans were so old and full of dry wood that in less than twenty minutes, most of them were sporting plumes of smoke.

The fire had spread to the tents. One of the big work hands who called himself Doc noted how fast the flames were spreading. He threw down his bucket and signaled to the other animal handlers. "Boys, we gotta get to the animals," he insisted, and several of the other hands nodded in agreement.

The animals were their bread and butter; without them, there was no show, no money, no reason for them to go on. They could replace the tents and caravans; they couldn't replace Worthington's exotic ménage of animals. The inhabitants of Tent City eventually gave up trying to save their homes and started racing toward the pavilion.

Adam dropped his own half-full bucket and slowly sank against one of the caravans which had only just begun to burn. It wasn't even hot yet. He noticed a mostly empty bottle of whiskey lying on the ground, abandoned by one of the workers when they ran off. He grabbed it up and drank down the last few swallows, then threw the bottle against the wall of the burning caravan opposite him— against the image painted there. It was Worthington's fat, smiling face, and it was on fire. On the ground between the two caravans lay his abandoned crossbow, and his last two bolts.

"Adam Bell, descendent of Robin of Locksley," he giggled, sounding like a madman. He knew where Worthington was headed, and he had every intention of catching up with the bastard and dragging his sorry ass down into hell with him.

| **32** |

Reign of Terror

By the time Anna and Syd reached the outskirts of the park, every caravan and tent was burning. Countless shabby little wooden structures had already been consumed and were nothing but piles of burning kindling, and the flames showed no sign of stopping.

A huge, black plume of smoke was rising high above Steeplechase Park, and the air was choked with smoke and burned stuff. Distantly—much too distantly—fire alarms were blaring as several fire pumpers headed for Coney Island. Rumor had it that New York had automated engines now, not just horse-drawn pumps, but Anna knew instinctively that their paltry little hoses would never be able to put out a fire of this size.

Syd stopped short, dragging Anna to a halt. Anna, coughing, threw up her hand to try and block the acrid smoke filling her lungs.

"We're never getting through that," he said, pointing at the wall of black smoke. "Sorry, Anna, I know you're worried about Adam, but he ain't worth both our lives."

There was no way she could argue with his logic. She didn't even try. Either Adam had gotten out or he was never going to do

189

so; either way, there was nothing they could do for him now. Black smoke surrounded them, turning noonday to midnight. It was suddenly so dark, Anna wasn't sure which direction they were going in anymore.

"You're right. How do we get out of here?"

Syd glanced around before pointing at a group of men who were running toward where she hoped the pavilion was located. Taking her hand, he started that way. As the two of them ran, trying to keep the smeary shapes of the men in their sights, something big brushed past Anna. She started and almost screamed as the thing squawked. She had a bad moment when she thought for certain that they were both being hunted by one of the Terror Birds, but then recognized the creature as an ostrich. An ostrich was racing in a panicked circle around the pavilion.

She was about to say as much to Syd when he said, "Ah…Christ, look out, Anna."

He yanked her into his arms, lifting her right off her feet, and twisted the both of them to one side as a pair of bellowing rhinoceroses raced past them, much too close for comfort. They had just narrowly missed colliding with the panicked animals.

Suddenly, they were surrounded on all sides by smeary, panicked, bellowing shapes. Animals. There were animals loose on the pavilion, running in every direction. Water buffalo were skittering across the porches of the shops, and birds like parrots and toucans were fluttering half-blind over the roofs.

As Syd set Anna down on her feet, a bad feeling permeated her whole being and made her stomach flip over. "Archie!" she screamed, looking around frantically for her little friend. "Archie, where are you?"

With a whistle, the little feathered dinosaur appeared out of the smoke, almost flying into Anna. She didn't care about his near collision; she was too happy to see he was all right. She opened her coat so Archie could hide in her inside pocket, away from the smoke. "The work hands...I think they're letting all the animals loose, Syd..."

"But not...them, right?" he said, turning to her. Despite the choking smoke, she could see his eyes were big and wild in his head. "I mean...they wouldn't do that...?"

She didn't know what they were capable of. All she knew was that the ringmaster they had seen earlier knew absolutely nothing about the prehistoric animals he was trying to educate the public on.

She took his hand. "I hope not. But we still have to check. What if they left the *Centrosauruses* behind?"

Syd gave her an incredulous look as he sidestepped being run over by a panicked giraffe galloping past. "I'd say that was a *good* thing, wouldn't you?"

"But they're not aggressive when they're not being provoked."

"Anna, for Christ's sake..."

She let go of his hand. "I don't expect you to understand."

He stuck his finger in her face. "I'm not putting us in danger because of some goddamned dinosaurs..."

"I'm not asking you to," she said when she realized the truth. She couldn't ask Syd to put his life at risk for this. If she did this, she would need to do it alone. She was the archaeologist, not him. This was her responsibility.

"And it's fine. I don't need your help! I do just fine on my own. Good day to you, sir!" Gripping the gun/sword close and sucking back on her tears, she took off toward the coliseum, trying not to look at all of the trampled and crushed bodies—human and animal— that littered the pavilion.

All the gawkers and workers had cleared the coliseum. As Anna made her way down the bleachers, she noticed the juvenile *Centrosaurus* racing in circles, crying pitifully while its mother trumpeted from a few yards away, still tied to a series of stakes pounded into the ground. The old bull, likewise, was still staked to the ground and moaning in misery. It looked like the workers had begun the process of releasing the dinosaurs, but then had abandoned the job mid-way.

As she hurried toward Mum and Baby, she noticed something out of the corner of her eye. She skidded to a halt about a hundred yards from the two dinosaurs, her heart thudding painfully hard in her chest.

"You bloody idiots!" she shouted when she realized what had happened.

Apparently, the workers had gotten the door of the giant bird-cage open, and Terror Birds were stalking around the edges of the coliseum, their hungry eyes tracking Mum and Baby. Several of those same workers now lay strewn across the ground, their bodies ripped to crimson ribbons by the talons and massive beaks of the carnivorous birds. There were shredded bodies and bloody, picked-over bones everywhere.

The birds, a half dozen in total, turned their greedy attention on Anna. She stiffened and felt her body solidify to the ground at the sight of them. She couldn't feel a thing. She couldn't even think. The biggest bird among them turned its head from side to side as it observed her. She saw its black, flint-like eyes, its vapid, soulless hunger. She could see her own terrified expression in its mirror-like eye as it gave her a long, hard, sideways look.

It did nothing at first. Just stood there on one leg, the other curled beneath its huge, shaggy body. It looked as much like a statue in a museum as anything real. Even the wind did not ruffle its coat of proto-feathers. Then its crimson crest slowly rose high into the air like a signal, reminding her of a pet Cockatoo when it's interested in something tasty. It opened its huge beak and let out a shrill hunting call.

Anna's entire body vibrated with the noise and her hair stood on end. Fearful tears filled her eyes and her breathing slowed all the way down, though her heart seemed to be trying to triphammer its way out of her chest.

The bird took one step toward her, then another. Anna wondered if this was what Edmond had seen in his last moments. Had he seen his own young, terrified face reflected in those demonic black eyes? Had he known he was going to die? Did he think of her, or their family, in those precious last seconds?

"Anna! Anna—your gun!" Syd was shouting at the top of his lungs.

Slowly, far too slowly, Syd's voice penetrated her haze. She realized the bird had been moving, subtlety making its way toward her a step at a time. Before she even knew it, the thing was only a few feet away. But so was Syd. He was standing at the top of the coliseum. He had come back for her!

The Terror Bird's eyes were glazed with lust and its beak was wide open as it lunged toward her.

"Anna! Your gun!"

The gun/sword. Yes. She felt nothing as she whipped the weapon out from under her coat, knocked off the safety, hefted it to her shoulder, and sighted down at the bird. It was so close, she could smell its meaty, musky breath, feel its heat. Without even blinking, she caressed the trigger and pulled it. The explosion deafened her momentarily…but her shot wasn't good and the bird kept coming.

It was almost upon her when its head suddenly exploded into bloody soup. Syd stood on the bleachers, his colt smoking. Anna almost cried with relief, then realized a second bird was almost at her shoulder. The first had merely been a distraction. She whipped around in the direction of the second one and jerked the trigger without looking.

Luck was on her side. Her shot obliterated its head. The other birds immediately noticed the blood and jumped on their brethren and started ripping their carcasses apart while Anna stood there, frozen in place.

Syd joined her on the floor of the coliseum in a matter of seconds, panting wildly. "Anna, you did good…real good," he said, moving toward her, his hand extended to push the weapon away.

She couldn't feel anything but cold, echoing terror washing over her.

"Anna?"

Something broke inside her. She felt that in some way, she had vindicated Edmond. She had made him proud. She erupted into sobs that shook her whole body. She sounded and looked ridiculous, she knew, but Syd didn't seem to care. He just grabbed her against the front of his cowhide coat and dragged her to the relative safety between the two *Centrosauruses*.

Once somewhat protected, he shushed her while he stroked away a few errant strands of hair cling to her cheeks. After a few seconds of him petting and holding her, he finally said in her ear, "We're getting out of here. All right?"

She nodded. Swallowed. "How?"

The Terror Birds shrilled their hunter's call into the smoky darkness descending over the fairgrounds. If they stepped out into the open, the birds would be upon them in seconds. But if they stayed here, they would eventually burn to death. There didn't seem to be any escape.

"We'll think of something," Syd said with a smirk. "We always do, don't we?"

| 33 |

Blood Money (II)

Worthington had the most elaborate caravan of all, of course—four times as large as the others, and outfitted with every possible modern convenience. When Carter Worthington traveled with his show, he traveled in style. And because he always parked it closest to the big top where he kept his most prized exhibit (whatever that was at the moment), it managed to be parked well away from the burning lot that was Tent City.

As Adam passed the big top, he could hear Worthington's security detail shouting and scrambling around nervously within the tent as they tried to decide how much of a threat the fire was. They had been ordered by Worthington to not leave the exhibit no matter what they saw or heard, but Adam sensed they were growing nervous. Additionally, he could hear something huge banging around the cage under the tent, snorting and stomping. Despite his blind rage and grief, he could feel a knot of worry squirming around his belly. Eyes smarting and lungs burning from all the smoke he'd inhaled, he moved past the tent and made a beeline for Worthington's caravan.

The door was wide open and he could hear Worthington rummaging around inside.

Panting like a dog, Adam hauled himself up the steps and through the door, still dragging the crossbow with him. He was tired and the crossbow felt like it was made of lead. His limbs ached and his chest burned. But he was determined to end the wanker inside.

Worthington, too, was coughing from smoke inhalation but valiantly trying to drag a heavy steamer trunk across the floor of his trailer. He'd drag it up by one end, shift it a foot, drop it, and then repeated the action. Adam wasn't fool enough to believe it held anything sentimental. The trunk contained a part of his fortune, because Worthington didn't give a damn about anything but money. It was only too bad that it took Adam this long to figure that out.

Raising his crossbow, Adam attempted to prime a bolt. It would have been smarter, cleaner, and faster to get a gun, he knew, but he wanted to shoot Worthington like the animal he was with the weapon he had used on the bloodthirsty predators of Blood Valley.

Worthington, however, looked up at the quiet little click of the crossbow. His bloodied face was stony hard, his teeth set in a grimace of desperation and pain. "What are you going to do, Adam, shoot me in the face with your toy? Shoot me in cold blood?"

"Why not?" Adam's voice was little more than a scorched whisper. All he could taste was smoke and tears. "You shot Will. You shot the only bloody thing that meant anything to me!" His hands were shaking with rage so badly that he had to keep drawing the crossbow back to the target at hand.

Worthington stood up and eyed him, raising his hands to show he was unarmed. The fact that he stood there, unafraid, a cocky smile on his face, only enraged Adam more. He wanted to see Worthington afraid and pissing his pants. He wanted to see the bastard begging on his knees as he shot him in his smug face.

"Please," Worthington spat in disgust. "You're not a cold-blooded killer, Robin of Locksley. You're a thief, a ne're-do-well, and a goddamn bunburry, but a killer? Come on. You're not going to shoot me and we both know that."

"You bastard," Adam hissed, shaking so badly his entire body seemed to vibrate. "You bloody bastard!"

"I'm sorry about Will, but look at it this way, Adam—now you're free to find the love of a good woman. In fact..." Worthington stopped and bent over to use a key on the steamer trunk. As Adam had suspected, it was full to brimming with wads of cash tied in neat bundles and bags of coins. He picked up a couple of bundles and offered them to Adam. "Take it. For whatever it was you two needed it for."

"I don't want your blood money!" Adam snarled through feral teeth. "I want Will back!"

"Consider this a partnership, then." Worthington picked up one of the heavy bags and un-cinched it. Inside was what looked like gold coins. Worthington showed Adam the coins. "You and I. We'll let all of this burn and start over. We'll go back to Blood Valley, find more animals. We'll be rich, Adam. We'll be the richest men in the world..."

Adam's aim was drifting again. He grabbed the crossbow in both hands and brought it back to bear on Worthington...whose face had begun changing. The color suddenly drained from it, and his look of avarice had been replaced with a more primal look of surprise...and fear.

Adam knew what the man was doing. He was trying to make Adam turn around. That's when Worthington would pull out a pistol and shoot him in the back...

The blasting shriek over his left shoulder was so loud, it momentarily deafened Adam. No longer worried about Worthington, he spun on his heel so he was facing the doorway...where a Terror

Bird was crouched on spring-like legs. Its massive, hooked beak was wide open and its head lowered. Adam was so close he could see all the way down its throat to its stinking gullet. With a cry, he swung the crossbow up, took aim, and fired, but too quickly in his panic.

The bolt went wild, missing the target by a mile, but at least the blast had the unexpected effect of making the bird shirk and withdraw momentarily. With a cry, Adam fell into the caravan on his arse end. The bird lunged, and Adam kicked the door closed on it. The wooden door smashed it in the face, enraging it. With a cry, Adam scuttled backward across the floor, away from the door, and smacked into the steamer trunk, behind which Worthington had taken cover.

Panting, almost choking on spit, smoke, and terror, Adam climbed shakily to his feet. He had no idea where the hell the bird had come from, but it was a good bet that however it had gotten loose, the others weren't far off. The bird thumped against the door, making him start, then withdrew, only to ram the door once more. The door buckled on its hinges, but held...for now.

"Shite!" Adam glanced around for an escape, spotting a small porthole window. Probably too small for a regular man to climb through, and definitely not Worthington, but he thought he might be small and scrawny enough.

He had almost reached it when another bird used its massive, hooked beak like a battering ram to smash the glass and poke its beak inside. Its gigantic maw opened wide open as it screamed in Adam's face, then snapped its jaws shut with the strength of a bear trap.

With a cry, Adam jerked back. The bird pushed its head against the porthole to better eye him, but there was no way it could fit its entire head inside the narrow opening.

Mumbling curses, Adam withdrew. The first bird again rammed the door, this time putting a crack in the wood. The second one rattled its oversized beak in the portal window. Meanwhile, Adam could hear the rap of clawed feet on the roof as a third bird danced on the roof.

It was only a matter of time before one or all of them got through. Mincing backward, away from the ravenous birds, Adam turned to the steamer trunk. Coins glittered on the floor where they had fallen when Worthington took cover. He had a flashback to his time at the nesting grounds of the Terror Birds, and with it the flash of a plan...of sorts.

"Worthington, get up!"

Worthington, crouched behind the steamer trunk, didn't move.

"I said get up!" Frustrated, Adam reached into the open trunk and grabbed up an open bag of coins. At that precise moment, the first bird smashed so hard into the door, it shattered into timber. The Terror Bird stepped into the doorway, making the whole caravan rock from its weight. Its head was low, crest high, its beak cracking wide open as it released its piercing hunting call.

"Wanker!" Adam shouted, throwing coins in its face. The bird squalled and shook its head, then noticed how shiny the coins were and started snapping at them as they flew past its face. Adam kept throwing coins, aiming for the door.

With a cry, the bird turned and jumped out of the caravan so it could chase the shiny coins rolling across the gravel. Grabbing a fresh sack of gold coins, Adam wasted no time rushing the door but only got a couple of feet when he felt resistance on the bag. He turned to find Worthington hanging onto it for dear life.

"Are you mad? Do you know how much money is there?"

"Let go, wanker!" Adam roared in his face. "Let go of it!"

"No!"

"You bloody fool!" said Adam, trying to wrest the sack away, but Worthington was as tenacious as terrier and refused to let it go. Adam yanked, and Worthington yanked it back.

I'm not going to die here today, killed by a bleedin' chook!

Before long, the two men were grappling and spitting obscenities in each other's faces as they twisted and turned in a ridiculous game of tug-of-war. To an outside observer, the two might have seemed to be ballroom dancing across the floor, the sack of coins vomiting a steady stream of gold onto the floor at their feet.

Finally, Adam's back hit the far wall of the caravan, and they could go no farther. Worthington, no flyweight, pressed Adam against the wall, pinning him with his bulk. He whipped out a nickel-plated Derringer from his boot.

"You worthless cur!" Worthington spittled in his face. He jerked the gun up so it was pointed at Adam's face. Adam, too angry to care about the danger, pushed it away. The gun twisted and turned as the two men wrestled for a better grip on it.

Finally, it went off.

| 34 |

Bloody Hell

Together, they worked on sawing through the ropes binding the old, scarred bull, Anna using the gun/sword and Syd using his Bowie knife, but the ropes were thick, the kind used on ships, and it felt like this was taking far too long.

"Anna, get a move on," Syd said. "Those dead birds aren't going to satisfy them for long."

"I know, Syd. I know," she answered, finally hacking wildly at the ropes. She heard one of the Terror Bird's crowing its hunting call. The sound shivered up her back. If she lived through this—which at this point seemed unlikely—the sound would haunted her dreams forever.

They had almost no time left. She hacked faster and faster while the bull *Centrosaurus* lay moaning in all his ropes. He looked thin and worn, both eyes running with a mysterious substance, and he seemed to be lying in a puddle of his own waste.

She started having doubts. What if he was too wounded to get up?

She couldn't worry about that. One crisis at a time.

Archie suddenly wriggled loose of her coat and landed on the ropes, pulling enthusiastically on strands of hemp. "That's right, Archie. Let's get him loose."

Archie squealed and pulled. Anna hacked. Suddenly, the rope split enough to unravel.

With a cry, Anna stepped back. But even though Syd had cut through the other rope binding him, the old bull just lay there, moaning. She felt like crying.

Something bumped her from behind and Anna swung around. She was face to face with Mum, who had managed to rip herself loose from of her own ropes. Her nasal horn alone was longer than Anna was tall. Anna almost screamed in fright.

She recalled the rhinoceros that had almost trampled her on the pavilion. She reminded herself that Mum was a wild and dangerous animal. Even if she didn't mean to, she was more than capable of harming Anna.

"H-hello, Mum," she stuttered, slowly putting a hand on the dinosaur's beaklike mouth. "I don't know if you understand me, but I mean you no harm."

The creature lowed in response but did not react in any violent way. Anna's eyes filled with tears. "I'm sorry this happened. I'm trying to fix it."

The creature blinked and bumped her, knocking Anna aside. It trotted up to the bull and nudged him. He just lay there, lowing softly in his throat.

Again Anna heard the remaining Terror Birds screaming as they started stalking around the edges of the coliseum. They were smart. They were being cautious around the larger animals, but Anna knew that wouldn't last. She remembered the enraged flock attacking Missus. When riled up by bloodlust, the Terror Birds made some questionable choices.

She got up and came around to face the bull. "Get up!" she shouted. Nothing. "Get up, please…they're coming!"

The creature just lay there.

She couldn't leave it to die. She couldn't leave *them* to die. She had failed Edmond. She would not fail Syd and these creatures. Taking a deep breath, she reassured her grip on the gun/sword and moved past Mum and out into the open even as Syd yelled for her to take cover, that she was a crazy woman. He was right; she was. Maybe she was crazy. But she was not going to be a coward.

The Terror Birds perked up and started gathering into a loose flock, all eyes pinned on Anna. One screamed and Anna screamed back at it, making it start and dance back a step in confusion.

"That's right, you oversized chicken!" she taunted it. "You can dish it out, but you certainly can't bloody take it!"

Baby lowed in terror, and the birds turned toward the sound. One lowered its head and raised its crimson crest, letting out a low, warbling noise of interest. Typical bully, always picking on the little bloke.

Anna stood her ground, sighting down the bird thought her scope, though her body was shaking so badly she had to reassure her grip on her weapon. This was it. She either killed the bird, or it killed her. She breathed in and out, in and out, and tried to slow her flitting heart and concentrate as she had when she was sighting down the bird dragging Syd away in Blood Valley, but it was diffi-cult. She felt like she might start hyperventilating at any moment.

The bird warbled, then charged her, moving incredibly fast as the Terror Birds were wont to do. As it filled the whole of her vision, Anna squeezed off a shot, but the bullet went wide, and she knew she had no time to try and re-aim.

The bird was almost upon her.

Taking the gun/sword in both hands, she slashed at it, trying to remember all her childhood training in rapier class, which she had been very good at—once.

The bird screamed and fell back onto the ground, a cut across its breast, but it wasn't a killing wound. It was bleeding, yes, but not bleeding fast enough. The bird shambled to its feet and shook itself, splattering her with its blood. It wasted no time lunging at her once more.

With a cry, Anna slashed at it, but the blade slid harmlessly off its gigantic beak. The bird twisted its head, knocking her down easily. Anna landed hard, the weapon skittering away. The bird squawked in delight and put one giant clawed foot upon her legs, pinning her to the ground. Its evil little eyes lit up with victory as it leaned down to open its gigantic maw.

Anna screamed again, so loud she didn't even hear the shot that obliterated the bird's head, turning it to bloody mush. The bird flopped over, and Anna sat up, staring at the sight before her.

Sydney Fly sat astride Mum's neck, just behind her frill, his long coat gently rustling in the wind, his smoking colt in one hand. Her heart thudded and sped up at the sight of him. She wished he didn't have that effect on her, but every time she looked at him, it was like everything in the universe disappeared around him.

"Anna!" he shouted. "Are you all right?"

She tottered uncertainly to her feet. "Yes...I think so." She looked down at all the bird blood all over her, then up at his dear face. The sight of him filled her heart to overflowing. "Thank you."

"Welcome, ma'am," he said with a small smirk, touching his cowboy hat. "Now get out of the way, woman!"

She was about to open her mouth and ask why when she heard a snort behind her. Starting, Anna turned round to face the gigantic bull, which was up on his feet at last. He was four times larger than an elephant, and standing, he towered over her at least a storey and a half. His gigantic nasal horn filled her whole field of vision as he let out a low bellow that made Anna lurch on her feet and send vibrations through the ground.

Anna waited, heart pounding, as the creature tottered on his feet and shifted side to side as he found his equilibrium. She held her breath as he turned his small, bright eyes on the Terror Birds who were edging closer, then twisted his gigantic, frilled head to the side to better see them. Anna thought she saw something very much like rage in them.

The bull snorted debris all over Anna and stomped the ground.

"I understand," Anna said and stepped out of his way.

Behind her came the now all-too-familiar hunting calls of two of the Terror Birds that had circled around behind them cleverly to take them all from behind. They were closing in, hungry enough to eye the bull with avid interest. The bull turned, lowered his head, lowed a warning, and lunged at the birds, moving faster than Anna would ever have believed for such a large animal.

Within seconds, he was in the midst of their numbers, stomping and thrashing them with his horn and tossing them high into the air. The Terror Birds never had a chance against the enraged bull.

Anna looked up at Mum, who was stomping and eyeing the remaining birds like she meant business.

Syd rode her like a king. "Get on!" he said, indicating Baby at her side. He was certainly more her size.

Laughing at the very idea, Anna climbed up onto Baby's foreleg the way she'd seen the circus performers climb up onto an elephant. Baby allowed her to clamber up the side of his body, using his frill for purchase, until Anna was astride his neck. "Syd!" she called over. "This is amazing!"

Syd pointed.

Anna turned in time to see the big bull stomping the bloody remains of the Terror Birds into a big red stain. Still bellowing, he lowered his head and charged the wall of the coliseum. The flimsy wooden structure proved to be no obstacle to the rampaging prehistoric bull, and it gave as easily as if it were made of papier-mâché.

Mum let out a bloodcurdling bellow and followed, with Baby close behind her. Anna and Syd held on for the ride of their lives.

Endgame

Covered in blood, bruises, and scrapes, Carter Worthington lifted the heavy steamer trunk off the ground, dragged it a few inches, then dropped it so he could rest. He repeated the motion, almost too tired to continue, but there was no way in hell he was going to leave half a million dollars to burn. He hadn't worked his entire life—rising up from nothing in the slums of this godforsaken city—for nothing.

His father had been a copper and a drunk who'd gambled away every penny he made, and if his mother even dared to protest, he would beat her silence with his billy club. The one time Worthington—who went by the name of Casey Wackett at the time—had found the courage to raise his hand to his father, his father had broken it in two places on him. The day his father died in a bar fight, a broken bottle in his liver, was the happiest day of Casey's life. Unfortunately, things only went downhill after that. His mother, having no means to support herself, was forced to sell herself on the street just so they could afford a squalid, rat-infested coldwater flat in the Five Points neighborhood.

He was twelve when a john cut his mother's throat in a stinking back alley. Not long after, with nothing to hold him in Five Points, Casey ran away and joined a pathetic little traveling circus and freak show. He did every job imaginable, no matter how lowly, though he found he had a particular affinity for the animals. He eventually came up with his own acts, many of them quite complicated, and by the time he was twenty years old, he owned that sad little show. From there, he had built his empire, one laborious step at a time. He wasn't going to finish it dirt poor and pathetic like his ne're-do-well father. He would rather die.

He dragged the steamer trunk a few more feet toward the coach house where he could hear the horses kicking and whickering as the fire grew ever closer. "Damnit…damnit, come on!" he cursed, dragging the trunk a few more feet before letting it drop down onto the sawdust-strewn pavilion. He was sweating and shaking from the effort.

He glanced around for his men, but everyone was either busy with letting the animals loose, trying to stifle the fire, or running away like the cowards they were. He was on his own. As always.

Swearing and shaking with rage, he raced to the coach house and threw the doors wide open. The horses went in a frenzy, kicking and bucking in their harnesses. Worthington knew why. Not more than a hundred yards away, he could hear the *Carnotaurus* rattling around her cage. Bars were shaken ominously, and the creature let out a frustrated huffing noise.

Worthington suddenly stopped and, ignoring the trunk of money lying in the middle of the pavilion for the moment, walked to the edge of the tent, throwing back a flap.

Inside, within the gigantic, specially made bamboo cage, the beast stalked around her small space, snapping and grunting with agitation. The cage, made of incredibly strong materials, had been specially designed by a Chinese architect that Worthington had hired. He'd wanted something special, something authentic-looking that conveyed a feeling of island exoticness in its detail. After all, appearances were everything in show business. But he also wanted it strong enough to hold a dinosaur. So far, it had done an excellent job.

The *Carnotaurus*, unlike the other animals who had been freed, was going to die in the carnivorous flames consuming Steeplechase Park. She was doomed. She had come to civilization only to be snuffed out by that old adversary: fire.

"Sorry, m'dear," Worthington said, watching her. He felt a pang. "Not much I can do for you."

The *Carnotaurus* who would have made him the richest man in the world whipped around, snapping her gigantic jaws together, and then turned her one lurid, working eye on him. In it, he could see a rage and frustration that he actually felt deep down in his bones. In that moment, he felt the same kinship with the beast that he had known years ago with the lions, tigers, and elephants in that old, dilapidated traveling carnival.

It did not deserve to die in the fire. None of these animals did. They had served him well. They deserved better than this.

The money didn't seem so important in that moment. Just them. The animals.

With tears in his eyes and resolution in his heart, Worthington made a decision, then. He would do something about his burning show. He'd fetch the hoses, help the firemen on the way. He'd free the rest of the animals, anything to make up for all of this.

Turning on his heels, he stepped outside the tent.

He didn't even see the old bull until it was upon him. Head lowered, festering, fly-filled eyes centered on its target, it barreled right at him in its desire for revenge. With its head so low, its horn filled Worthington's entire field of vision.

He never felt a thing as the tip of the horn pierced his chest, impaling him upon it like an insect on an entomologist's pin, and he felt nothing further as the old bull *Centrosaurus* collided with the bamboo cage and lifted its head up with a roar of war, its enormous, locomotive-like power ripping the bamboo cage to flimsy pieces that fluttered down like flotsam around the two behemoths.

Worthington's body was crushed beneath thousands of pounds of debris and would not be found until days later, after everything had come to pass, and after almost everyone had assumed that he'd run off to South America in defeat.

With no family to claim his body, and no friends to care about his passing, Carter Worthington's body would eventually be interred in a common grave. No mourners attended the ceremony, not even his former employees, though upon the memorial headstone, someone eventually chiseled the epitaph *Forsan miseros meliora sequentur.*

For those in misery perhaps better things will follow.

* * *

The *Centrosaurus* bull and the *Carnotaurus* female had been enemies for millions upon millions of years. Their enmity was as old as the hills that surrounded Blood Valley and as deep as the river that cut a primordial path through it. The moment the *Carnotaurus* was free, she lunged at her old enemy, but the bull, having been kept in restraints for months while his rage festered, was strong and angry and, most frightening of all, dying. He had nothing to lose.

The two titans clashed. The bull's horn grazed the *Carnotaurus's* belly, but she was quick, and millions of years of evolution had carved her into a streamlined killing machine. In seconds, she was upon him, her taloned hind foot scraping against the bull's frill while she leaned down to bite at the bony protrusion. The *Centrosaurus* roared and tossed his head. The motion knocked them both over, and within seconds, the two giants were rolling along the pavilion, crushing the little shops that had existed there for decades and the replica of Big Ben that had been a star attraction of Steeplechase Park almost from the beginning.

The building crumbled down upon the two animals as they wrestled, locked in mortal combat. They smashed Carter Worthington's steamer trunk to fragments and his money went flying high like a giant flock of birds, which attracted the immediate attention of a pair of Terror Birds who had been hunting along the fringes of the burning pavilion. They had been fighting over a few human bones, but when they saw the money flying through the burning debris rising high into the sky, they screeched and raced toward the two battling dinosaurs.

The *Carnotaurus* delivered a fierce bite to the back of the old bull's neck. The bull screamed and swung around, thumping his long, powerful tail into the *Carnotaurus's* side. Missus bellowed as she was knocked down. The bull turned sharply, and, with a roar, charged the downed *Carnotaurus*, sinking his nasal horn into his enemy's belly. Missus screamed in pain and rage and clamped her great jaws down on his frill, ripping away bone and flesh. The bull raised his head as he roared in pain and Missus grabbed his horn in her teeth, shaking the creature side to side and finally ripping his nasal horn loose in a geyser of blood and gristle as the two creatures proceeded to try to kill each other.

By the time the Terror Birds arrived, bits of burning money were floating down around them, and they proceeded to chase the shiny gold coins that were rolling across the abandoned pavilion.

| **36** |

Riding the Dinosaur

The remaining Terror Birds on the pavilion scattered as Anna and Syd cut a swath through their numbers. Syd was holding on like the cowboy he was, while Anna, hat in hand, was whooping and yeehawing as best she could in an effort to frighten the birds standing in their way. Some were too arrogant—or too hungry—to move. They just stood there, heads down, beaks wide open and screaming as they were run down by the galloping *Centrosauruses*. And Mum and Baby...well, they took no prisoners.

Driven by the siren song of freedom, Mum barreled down the promenade with Baby close behind her. Anna urged him on, waving her big, feathered hat around, her hair falling down around her sweaty face. She didn't care.

Mum trumpeted and tossed her head like a gigantic rhinoceros, her nasal horn thrashing side to side, scattering more birds, who turned to follow them, though they weren't nearly fast enough—or strong enough—to stop Mum.

Ahead, a group of people were cowering inside one of the empty exhibit coves while Terror Birds stalked toward them.

"Look, Syd!"

Syd leaned forward and shouted that Mum should go get 'em. As if she could understand them, Mum turned all her fury on the birds, racing right into their fray and tossing her head, throwing squealing Terror Birds in every direction. One came down upon Mum's back, but Anna saw it and, clinging to Baby's frill with one hand, used the other to aim the gun/sword at the bird and shoot it off Mum's arched back, the bullet passing by within inches of Syd's ear.

"Hell, Anna!" he bellowed angrily. "Watch what you're doing, you crazy woman!"

"Didn't hit you, did I?" She grinned as she urged Baby onward down the pavilion where people were racing in every direction. Many looked injured and had scratches and bleeding wounds. Where Anna saw a Terror Bird popping up, she commanded Baby on, and Baby compiled by turning his wild rage on the bird in their path.

Within minutes, they had cleared most of the pavilion and the Terror Birds lay dead or injured. Ahead, lay the burning collection of caravans. The fire had spread substantially, and in the coming darkness of nightfall, the burning big top tent stuck out like a fiery beacon. Bodies lay everywhere, the tattered remains of the Terror Birds' savage attacks. It only spurred Anna on, made her want to wreak an even greater vengeance on the birds that had done this.

In the dark, she almost didn't see Missus until she rose up before them, dark against the burning tent. She had been bent over this whole time, feasting wildly upon the crumpled remains of the dead bull. Anna saw that clearly now, and it felt like her heart had been kicked up into her throat at the sight. The *Carnotaurus's* face and jaws were slathered with gore, and her one eye rolled wildly in her head. Despite the way she had been gluttonously stuffing her jaws, she looked on Mum with an endless and terrible hunger.

Mum halted dead in her tracks and stomped her feet in warning. Behind her, Baby lowed in fear. Mum grew wilder as the sound increased, but Missus was blocking their path to freedom. Shifting her weight from foot to foot, Mum let out a disgruntled snort.

Syd slipped off Mum's back and hurried round to Anna, still sitting atop Baby. "This is our stop," he said, lifting his arms to her.

Anna slid down the side of Baby's side and let him catch her. "Mum," she said with concern. It was obvious the *Centrosaurus* was preparing for battle with the *Carnotaurus*, but Syd held her back.

"I'm afraid that in this situation, Anna, you can't do anything."

"You're right, of course." She could not fight this battle for Mum. She was helpless in this situation.

Turning to the man holding her so securely in his arms, she smiled. "Let's go, Mr. Darcy. Let's get out of here."

* * *

Missus wasted no time charging Mum, but Mum had proven herself no shrinking violet. Instead of retreating, Mum stood her ground. In the seconds before Missus was upon her, Mum turned sideways and scraped her nasal horn along Missus's belly as the *Carnotaurus* roared past. Missus's momentum carried her down onto her face on the pavilion, but she was up and on her feet in seconds, though there was now more than one deep gouge in her belly—the one she had just received from Mum as well as an earlier injury she had more than likely received from the old bull.

Roaring in pair and rage, Missus leaped upon Mum's back, snapping and biting. Her massive jaws clacked down upon Mum's frill, and Mum responded with a trumpet of pain and began to twist in circles as she attempted to dislodge Missus from her back. Missus, though, would not let go, and the longer their battle went on, the more blood flew and the quicker Anna felt her stomach falling. Standing on the edge of the pavilion beside Syd, she mashed her hands over her mouth to keep from sobbing and simply watched as the two animals crashed over only a few hundred feet away.

She was still staring even as Syd dragged her out of harm's way.

The two animals rolled over and over and started kicking and biting. Missus was larger than her foe, but she was also injured from her previous fight with the old bull, and when Mum managed to find her feet, which was easier for her as a bipedal animal, she spared Missus no quarter and tore her horn through the tender flesh along Missus's side. Missus roared and rolled over in the debris and blood, eventually coming up on her feet, though it was obvious she was mortally wounded.

She crouched there, panting and eyeing her foe. She was covered head to foot in blood, and she looked like she had lost some teeth during their clash. Mum rocked unsteadily on her feet, clearly tiring from the battle. Yet Missus's greedy gimlet eyes shone. She looked ready to spring, when a cry from Baby drew her attention.

Spotting a much easier meal, a more vulnerable target, Missus let out a hunting call as she lunged for Baby. Her greed was her undoing. By doing that, she had fully exposed herself. Mum let out a snort like an angry bull, dropped her head down, and charged Missus.

The *Centrosaurus* sank her nasal horn deep into the larger predator's belly. The blood was astronomical and sprang skyward at least a hundred feet, raining down upon Anna and Syd as they clutched each other. Missus screamed in a way that Anna had never heard before and toppled over.

She lay there, kicking and quivering for some minutes until the last few drops of life ran out of her body. Then, with a roar of triumph, Mum turned and raced toward the boardwalk, Baby at her side. Lowing in unison, they galloped down the sandy banks of the shore and into the fresh, frothy night surf of the Atlantic.

| 37 |

Night Tide

While firemen worked at dousing the flames eating a giant big, black heart through Coney Island, Anna and Syd stumbled together down the banks of the shore and waded knee-high into the Atlantic tide to watch Mum and Baby frolicking in the surf.

Anna was shaking—from cold or shock, she had no idea. Syd, noticing, took off his greatcoat and wrapped it around her shivery shoulders.

"Thank you, Sheriff," she said, clutching the collar around her neck. Once, in another life, she might have given it back to him, terrified it made her seem a weak, wilting woman, but she'd since decided there was still room for a little bit of chivalry in her world. At least, there was if it came from Sydney Fly.

After a few minutes of watching the dinosaurs play, Anna felt a smile spread across her sooty face. She was surprised to still be able to find one through all this terrible mess. "Do you think we can convince the authorities to take Mum and Baby back to Blood Valley?"

Syd reached up and gave Archie a pet as the little dinosaur alighted on his shoulder and warbled in wonder. "I think we can try and persuade them. It shouldn't be that difficult, in light of everything that's happened tonight."

Anna nodded, then swallowed against the lump in her throat. So many had perished because of Worthington. And because of *her*. Because she had insisted on finding her brother—who had died long before she ever set foot in America.

Again, she swallowed. If she could take it all back…if she could do something…

A husky cough made Anna turn her head toward the barnacle-covered pilings under a nearby pier. The cough came again, hoarser this time.

"A little help here, please."

"Adam?" she said before breaking away from Syd and crashing through the water until she was under the pier. She crouched down beside the dark figure there. Yes, it was him.

It was Adam, half on, half off shore, sitting with his back to a piling, a giant crossbow in his lap. He was shivering and soaking wet, with a bloody gunshot hole in his upper thigh. His head was bowed and his face pale, but at least he was alive.

"Adam!" She threw herself on him, perhaps too harshly because he winced. "Sorry…are you all right?"

Looking like a half-drowned rat, he shifted his back against the pilings and nodded. There were dark circles under his eyes, bruises and burns on his face and hands, and he looked like he had literally been through the gates hell. "I think so…bloody hell, I don't know."

His wound looked deep, but not fatal. Anna was about to rip a strip off her skirt for a tourniquet when she saw his eyes light up and he straightened as he lifted the crossbow in his lap to the level of his shoulder. It was already primed with a bolt, and all Anna could think of was Syd standing behind her.

"Adam, no…!" she shouted, but he fired too quickly.

"Syd!" she screamed, spinning around, but Syd wasn't there. Instead, she saw a Terror Bird, its jaws wide open, as it dropped with a plash into the water under the pier and start to bleed out, a bolt in its side. It kicked and squawked for a few seconds before falling silent and letting the tide take it out to sea.

"Wanker chook!" Adam spat.

Syd appeared beside her. "It looks like Adam will be just fine, but let me fetch a medic. I'm sure there's one around here somewhere."

Adam clutched Anna's arm. "Don't bring them, please," he pleaded. "If the police find me..." He shook his head. "I can't go to prison. *Please.*"

He looked terrified—and so very young.

It broke her heart. Anna smiled as she scooted down. "Fine. We won't tell anyone. Syd and I will take care of that wound."

Syd gaped. "What? I am not—!"

Anna held up a hand to hush him and Syd sighed. He knew he wouldn't win this one anymore than he'd won any of the others.

"Thanks," Adam said, turning his attention on Mum and Baby who were tossing sea foam over each other. His eyes darkened. "We have to make certain this never happens again, Anna. We have to make certain no one ever removes them from their environment ever again. Educate them."

"Yes," Anna agreed as she and Syd came around to hoist Adam to his feet between them. "Educate them."

She, like the others, turned to watch the dinosaurs playing in the surf. "That's what archaeologists do."

The Beginning
The Archaeologists will return in
Titian Island

ABOUT THE AUTHOR

K.H. Koehler is the author of various novels and novellas in the genres of horror, SF, dark fantasy, steampunk, and young and new adult. She is the owner of KH Koehler Books and KH Koehler Design, which specializes in graphic design and professional copy-editing. Her books are widely available at all major online distributors and her covers have appeared on numerous books in many different genres. Her short work has appeared in various anthologies, and her novel series include *The Kaiju Hunter*, *A Clockwork Vampire*, *The Nick Englebrecht Mysteries*, and *The Archaeologists*. She is the author of multiple Amazon bestsellers and was one of the founders and chief editors of KHP Publishers, which published genre fiction from 2001 to 2015. She has over fifteen years of experience in the publishing industry as a writer, ghostwriter, copyeditor, commercial book cover designer, formatter, and marketer. Visit her website at https://khkoehler.net.

www.ingramcontent.com/pod-product-compliance
Lightning Source LLC
Chambersburg PA
CBHW012036140726
47990CB00010B/3248